Curse of the ChupaCabra

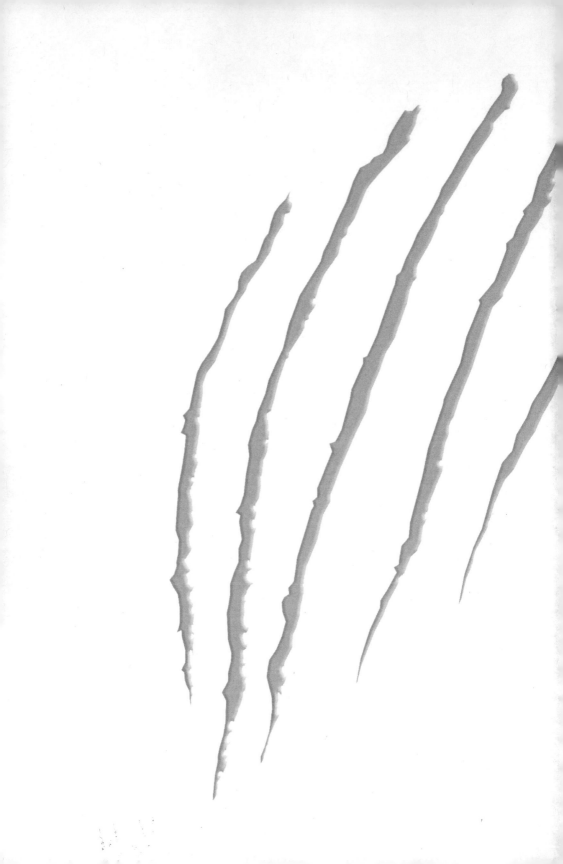

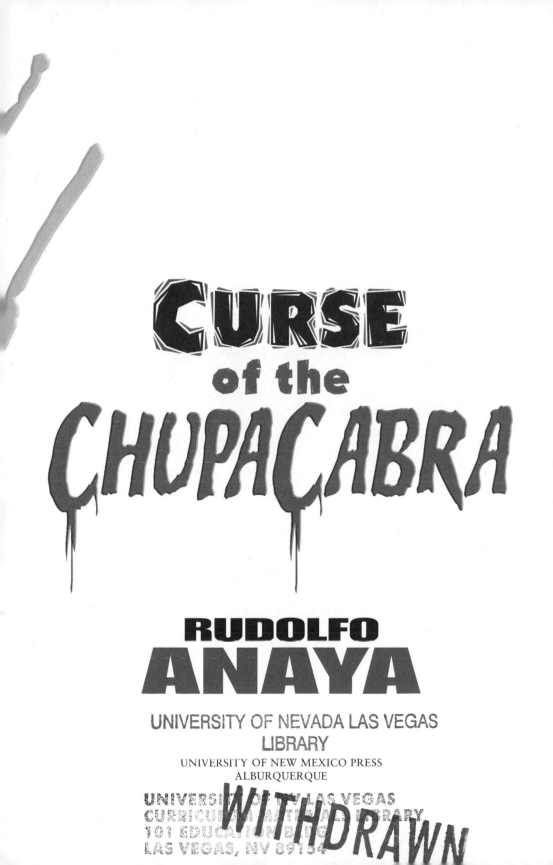

CURSE
of the
CHUPACABRA

RUDOLFO ANAYA

UNIVERSITY OF NEW MEXICO PRESS
ALBURQUERQUE

YEAR   PRINTING
10 09 08 07 06   1 2 3 4 5

Library of Congress Cataloging-in-Publication Data

Anaya, Rudolfo A.
  Curse of the ChupaCabra / Rudolfo Anaya.
      p. cm.
  Summary: Professor Rosa Medina, a folklorist researching
the ChupaCabra, goes to Mexico to track down recent sightings
of the creature which kills its victims, particularly goats, by
sucking their brains out.
  ISBN-13: 978-0-8263-4114-3 (cloth : alk. paper)
  ISBN-10: 0-8263-4114-4 (cloth : alk. paper)
  [1. Chupacabras Fiction. 2. Monsters Fiction.
3. Drug abuse—Fiction. 4. Hispanic Americans—Fiction.
5. Mexico—Fiction.] I. Title.
  PZ7.A5186Cur 2006
  [Fic]—dc22
                                    2006017385

Book design and composition by Damien Shay
Body type is Sabon 10.5/15
Display is Carver ICG, Protest, and Impact

This book is dedicated to all those seeking a path of liberation.

We are losing so many of our young people to drugs. If we are to save our youth, the fight to get drugs out of our communities must intensify. We cannot afford to lose our best minds and the future they represent.

Over the years I have received many letters from Chicano pintos in prisons from California to Texas. They all ask me to send them books that deal with their history and culture. They realize that getting separated from the values of their ancestors was one reason they went down dead-end streets. When our youth lose touch with their roots, they often turn to drugs.

We need to get the young back into the fold of their history and culture. We need to help them develop pride and a *si se puede* attitude.

Yes, complex social issues surround the world of drugs, but one thing is clear: drugs enslave. There are dedicated workers willing to help those who want to break the chains. I hope I contribute a small part to the effort by writing this story.

CHAPTER ONE

Jungle vines and tree branches bloodied Rosa Medina's face as she dashed down a dark path. Behind her the ChupaCabra was closing in. She could feel the hot breath of the beast on her neck. A horrifying scream filled the air as the monster pounced on her. As she went crashing to the ground Rosa felt the monster's sharp claws dig into her back.

A terrified Rosa sat up so fast she almost jumped out of bed. The phone was ringing. Her bedroom was dark; only the window curtains stirred in the breeze.

"Thank God," she whispered. It was a nightmare. She glanced at her bedside clock. Six AM. Who would be calling this early?

Still trembling, she picked up the phone and mumbled a hello.

"Rosa, it's me, Alfredo. There's been an incident!"

Rosa turned on the bedside lamp. Alfredo Vargas was a friend from Lago Negro, a village in Mexico. An incident could only mean that ChupaCabra had struck again.

"Did you hear me, Rosa?"

"Yes, yes, go on Alfredo."

Three goats had just been found dead in the jungle above the village, Alfredo reported.

"Where?"

"By the lake. One of the campesinos went there to look for his goats and found them dead."

"Does Herminio know?"

"Yes. He has not seen the goats. But he believes it is ChupaCabra. Everyone in the village says it is ChupaCabra. The people are frightened."

"Have the dead goats been moved?" Rosa asked.

"No. They're in the jungle. The men do not want to go there. They are afraid."

"Good. Don't touch anything. I'm making reservations right away. If I can get a morning flight I should be there this afternoon. Tell Herminio."

"Yes, we will be waiting for you," Alfredo replied, and the phone went dead.

Rosa bolted into action. She called José Bustos, her graduate teaching assistant at Cal State L.A. Rosa had shared her ChupaCabra research with him, and he had become an enthusiast. Now they had an incident they could investigate, and José's training in photography would be invaluable. The villagers said the ChupaCabra often returned to its kill. Maybe this time they could photograph the beast.

"José, buenos días. It's me, Rosa."

"Rosa? What time is it?"

"What are you doing for spring break?"

"Doing? You know what I'm doing. I'm writing the paper I owe Dr. Cantú."

"Want to go to Mexico?" Rosa asked, and explained what had happened.

"Of course I want to go!" José replied. "The paper can wait. I'll get my stuff together."

"Bring your cameras for night photos," Rosa said. "We will be in the jungle."

"You got it," José replied. "Pick me up."

Next she called AeroMexico. There was a nine o'clock flight out of LAX direct to Puerto Vallarta. She made reservations for two.

As the plane flew south, Rosa recalled the events that had brought her originally to Puerto Vallarta.

Two years ago she had finished her Ph.D. at Santa Barbara. The university had the best Chicano Studies faculty in the country. After graduation she had been hired to teach at Cal State. Literature was her field, and as a young assistant professor she knew she should be concerned with publishing her research, but she was also fascinated by folklore. Her deepest interest was in the lore of the ChupaCabra. She had documented every report of the mysterious creature. ChupaCabra sucked the blood of small animals, usually goats and chickens people kept in their backyards. Sometimes it killed dogs.

Some said the creature had first appeared in Puerto Rico. Puerto Ricans joked that ChupaCabra had gotten a passport and flown to Mexico. From there the elusive creature migrated north, or so the stories said. People swore ChupaCabra had killed backyard animals in Texas, California, New Mexico, and one as far north as South Chicago. Only one incident of ChupaCabra attacking humans had been recorded, and that was in Lago Negro, where last year the creature had killed a campesino hunting iguanas in the jungle.

Two years ago during her job interview at Cal State, one crusty, old professor had teased her about her work on ChupaCabra. A scholar in the literature of the Puritans, he clearly hated anything that had to do with ethnic studies.

Rosa talked enthusiastically about her interest. She had collected Dracula stories and the folktales of other creatures known as bloodsuckers. She also kept files of werewolf stories, Bigfoot sightings, even the Loch Ness monster. Even the Gilgamesh epic, which dated 2,700 years before Christ, featured Humbaba, the archetypal forest monster whom Rosa considered the original ChupaCabra.

The old professor interrupted her. "So the ChupaCabra is also the troll beneath the bridge the three billy goats had to cross."

"Exactly!" Rosa replied. "A troll fits the definition of ChupaCabra. A forest monster, hiding in the dark, ready to kill the billy goats. It's a motif in folktales around the world. These creatures have appeared in folk stories for ages."

Dr. Cantú, an expert on Chicano literature, spoke in her defense.

"I find the relationships you're making fascinating," he said. "Our Anglo colleagues must acknowledge the myths from the Latino south are penetrating the American consciousness. La frontera between Mexico and the U.S. should be a mirror where we see each other's reflection, not a wall. Our students need to learn the mythology of the south. We must know not only Grimm's fairy tales but also the legends of the Aztecs. As you say, Rosa, the ChupaCabra has its antecedents in world myths."

Rosa smiled. Someone understood her.

But the old professor shook his head.

"Dr. Medina, you have excellent credentials, but I suggest you stick to literature. The ChupaCabra, the goat sucker, is only a figment of the popular imagination, like the Llorona stories my Mexican American students tell me. I listen, but I know there is no Llorona."

No Llorona! Rosa almost exploded. Of course la Llorona exists! Every Mexican child had heard a version of the crying woman's story. Archetypal images were as real as the wart on the nose on the old professor. Stories were real; la Llorona was real whether one saw her or not. She lived in the soul of the people. Rosa's research had traced la Llorona from Aztec mythology through her various forms in Mexican folklore and into her appearance as goddess in the paintings and stories of contemporary Chicanas.

Rosa fumed. The pinche professor was saying there was no Llorona! What did he know!

The professor winked. "Well, you've got the job, but take some friendly advice, stick to the subject." He left the room, leaving behind a deflated Rosa.

The ChupaCabra was real; it left dead animals behind. ChupaCabra was like la Llorona and el Cucúi. Creatures of the dark night, they lived in the stories of the people.

But the stories from the Latino south were new in el norte. The border remained a wall, not a mirror. American students studied the myths recounted in the *Iliad* and the *Odyssey*, not the creatures from Mexican mythology.

By noon the plane was touching down in Puerto Vallarta. Rosa hurried onto the tarmac, searching for Herminio among the eager taxi drivers who pressed forward. Herminio lived in Lago Negro but drove into Puerto Vallarta every day to earn his living as a taxista.

Lago Negro had once been a quiet, pleasant village, but now, Rosa had heard from Alfredo, strange things were happening. Foreigners had moved in. Mafiosos, the people said. They dealt in contrabanda. Drugs. She hoped to learn more from Herminio and his wife, Lupe.

The ChupaCabra was known to return to the scene of its most recent kill. Tonight Rosa and José would be waiting, hoping to photograph it.

CHAPTER TWO

"Herminio!" Rosa shouted when she spotted her friend. He was at the end of the line, finishing his lunch and washing it down with a refresco. She and José hurried toward the taxi.

"Rosa, como estas? Que gusto me da. Alfredo told me you would be on this flight."

"I'm glad to see you, Herminio. This is my friend, José. He's a photographer." The two men shook hands.

"Can you drive us?"

"Of course. Con mucho gusto," Herminio replied. "I've been waiting. Alfredo had to work. He could not come. Lupe will be very glad to see you." He loaded Rosa's bag and José's camera equipment into his taxi.

They were quickly on their way out of the city and on the narrow road that led to Lago Negro.

"Tonight you and José will come and eat with us. Lupe will prepare some of those tacos de pescado you love. She is so excited."

"Thank you, Herminio. It would be a pleasure, but this evening we have to go into la selva."

Herminio frowned. "To see the evil work of the ChupaCabra. It is not safe, Rosa."

Something in his voice told her that if ChupaCabra had struck once, it could strike again. She had heard the same warning in Alfredo's voice. Something they didn't understand was lurking in the jungle.

"I'll be careful. And José is with me."

"We can handle anything," José responded. "Besides, taking photos of a couple of dead goats doesn't seem dangerous."

"It is not just dead goats," Herminio replied. "The way they were killed is mysterious."

"You mean the goatsucker," José said. "I'm from East L.A., señor. I can handle anything."

"I brought a small regalito for Lupe," Rosa interrupted, reaching into her purse for a small package.

"Ah, Rosa, you are too kind. She will be so happy. As you know, things are difficult. The government keeps telling us things are getting better, but the price of tortillas keeps going up. The politicians and the big shots make money, but not the working man. I tell you, those muchachos in Chiapas did the right thing."

Herminio stopped at the only hotel in the village. The dilapidated El Perico hotel had only four rooms to rent and a small open-air dining terrace with two tables. Past the palm trees lay a fabulous view of the Pacific Ocean.

Today two men sat drinking beer at one of the tables. They turned to study Rosa and José.

"See the tuerto," Herminio whispered as he opened the trunk.

Rosa looked at the heavy-set, one-eyed man.

"Calls himself El Jefe. He's bad news."

"I'll stay out of his way," Rosa said. "We came to do a scientific study, not politics."

"I don't like it," Herminio said. "The selva is not safe." He nodded toward the jungle that covered the slope of the mountain.

"The ChupaCabra," she said.

Herminio shrugged. "Something muy mal is haunting our village. Look at our streets. They are nearly empty. The people are leaving. The campesinos who remain are afraid to go into the hills with their goats. Bad times have come to Lago Negro."

"We'll be careful," Rosa replied. "Alfredo will be with us."

"Yes, he is a good man."

Making his farewells, Herminio got into his taxi and disappeared around the bend in the road. He lived on the far side of the village.

As Rosa and José entered the terrace, El Jefe stood and blocked Rosa's path. "Just a minute señorita. What is your business here?"

Rosa, annoyed at his arrogance, calmly answered. "My business is to rent rooms for the night. Since you are not the hotel manager that is none of your business."

The man frowned. "You think you are so smart. We don't want pochas like you snooping."

Pocha? Rosa's anger flared. She had never been called a pocha! She was born in Santa Fe, New Mexico, and she spoke Spanish fluently. She had visited Mexico many times; one summer she had studied in Cuernavaca. She had many friends in Mexico.

"I'm not a pocha and I'm not snooping," Rosa replied, trying to keep the anger under control. "I'm here to do research—"

"Research!" El Jefe interrupted her. "We know you have been here before. You believe the stories of the campesinos, don't you? Those ignorant people don't know anything! They should know enough to stay out of the jungle."

"They have made a living in the selva all their lives," Rosa answered. "Why should they leave their land?"

"I warn you, we don't need you norteamericanas making trouble," El Jefe said threateningly. "Leave now. Go to Puerto Vallarta. Act like the other turistas. Then go home."

He turned abruptly, signaled to his crony, and the two left the cafe. They got into a large SUV and roared away, leaving a cloud of dust hanging in the street.

"Norteamericana! Pocha!" Rosa snorted. "Who does he think he is!"

"He's one ugly hombre," José said. "But why would he threaten you?"

"Alfredo said drug dealers have moved in," Rosa replied. She looked up the mountain slope. "But why here? There's nothing here, except—"

"ChupaCabra," José finished her thought.

"It doesn't make sense," Rosa said. "Anyway, he's not going to keep me from documenting this new lead."

"That's the spirit, profe," José said. "I'm right behind you."

She turned and entered the hotel lobby. José followed, lugging his camera equipment.

CHAPTER THREE

Rosa and José sat on the hotel terrace enjoying a refresco and the sun setting over the Pacific. The cirrus clouds racing overhead glowed in feathery mauves and oranges.

"Hard to imagine such a peaceful place is the haunt of the ChupaCabra," José remarked.

"There's something more than ChupaCabra," Rosa replied, motioning to the jungle that rose up the side of the mountain.

"Why a place like this? Seems isolated."

"Used to be," Rosa replied. "Now there are men like El Jefe hanging around. And scaring the villagers away."

Just then Alfredo drove up. Like many other natives, he worked at the hotels along the beaches. He greeted Rosa with an embrace.

"Rosa, I'm so glad to see you. Sorry I'm late. Cruise ships arrived today. The hotel was full. Como estas?"

"Estoy bien, y tu? And you're not late. Mira, te presento mi amigo." Rosa introduced José.

"Hey, homes, howsitgoin'?"

"Homes?" Alfredo looked puzzled, thinking José had not heard his name correctly. "Alfredo," he said.

"Yeah, homes. Alfredo."

"Oh, I get it," Alfredo said. "Homeboy!" He gave José the amigo handshake.

"Orale!" José smiled.

"We're ready if you are," Rosa said.

"Pues, vamos."

They loaded their equipment in backpacks and Alfredo led them up a trail into the jungle. The green shadows grew deeper. Rosa pointed to a large iguana scurrying up a coconut palm.

"Do they bite?" José asked. This was his first visit into the jungle and he was fascinated. He kept photographing every animal that scurried across their path.

"No," Rosa replied. "They're friendlier than the Jefe hanging out at the hotel. What's going on, Alfredo?"

"Jefe and his gang are narcotraficantes. Best to stay out of their way."

"And the police?" Rosa asked.

Alfredo shrugged. "The police do nothing. You know, they get a mordida and turn their backs."

It was not news to Rosa that the drug traffickers paid off the police. Every time the DEA, in cooperation with honest Mexican police, arrested a kingpin of one of the drug cartels, a new boss quickly stepped in and created a new organization. Drug use in the states created one of the most lucrative markets in the world.

Rosa thought of the young people she was mentoring in L.A. Once a week she drove into East L.A. to meet with four kids at Self-Help Graphics. She was beginning to learn the way drugs attacked the Latino community. Young Chicanos in the barrios were targeted by pushers. Once hooked, the kids lost hope. The oppressive poverty in the barrios didn't help.

The students she tutored had been into drugs and gangs, but were now struggling to find their way out of that world. Beautiful kids with beautiful souls, if only someone helped them.

Chuco, who thought he was the baddest, was now doing great in the program. Mousey, who had joined a gang for protection, was ready to apply to a junior college. Leonora, whom everybody called Leo, was a beauty. She was headed for modeling school. One day, Rosa was sure, Leo would find herself in movies. And Indio, a young Navajo from New Mexico, had not touched drugs in a year.

So once a week Rosa drove down Avenida César Chávez to meet with them and teach them how to write. They read and discussed books and wrote their impressions. In a short time their improvement had been phenomenal, and Rosa looked forward to her meetings with them.

How different her upbringing had been in Santa Fe. The city was still small enough to give her a sense of community, a sense of belonging. Her tíos, tías, and many cousins lived in town. The extended family usually knew what the young were doing and that helped keep them in line. But even in the bucolic villages of northern New Mexico drug usage was creating devastation.

"Aquí estamos," Alfredo called.

In half an hour they had reached a large clearing in the jungle where Rosa saw the dead goats, a female and her kid. Something in the dense atmosphere, Rosa thought, smelled like sulfur.

"They belonged to Don Jacinto," Alfredo explained, "but he hasn't been back since he found them. He came to the village and told everyone the ChupaCabra had killed his goats. Nobody would come here. And look closely. The vultures have not eaten the goats. Why?"

Yes, why? Rosa thought as she placed her backpack on the ground. The evening shadows were thick; the jungle was closing in on them.

"Where is the lago?" José asked.

"Muy cerca," Alfredo replied, pointing at a dark path over-hung with vines. "The village gets its name from the lake. Once people used the waters for medicine. Now the lake stinks. Something contaminated it. Everything has changed."

"Cars have been here," Rosa said. "There are tire tracks."

"Chingao!" Alfredo exclaimed. "Somebody is using the old trail as a road. Why drive up here?"

"Aquí!" José called. Rosa and Alfredo hurried to his side. A large swath of the clearing was burned and trampled. The faint smell of diesel fuel laced the air.

"What do you think?" Rosa asked.

"I didn't know there was a road here," Alfredo replied. "And something burned the grass! Some of the campesinos say the ChupaCabra is a creature from outer space. People see lights at night and they say it is a spaceship that lands. They hear strange sounds. It has frightened the old people."

"I'm sure there's a logical explanation," José said. "I'm going to set my camera up at the edge of the clearing. If a ChupaCabra comes tonight, I'll get it on film. That will solve the mystery."

"You're going to stay here tonight?" Alfredo asked, incredulous.

"That's what I came for," José replied. "It's a warm night, I've got my granola bars and a poncho in case it rains. I'm good."

"Estás loco!" Alfredo exclaimed.

"No," José replied. "Not loco, just curious. If the ChupaCabra returns to feast on goat meat, I plan to photograph it."

"But it's dangerous!"

"Come on, Alfredo. An animal that kills goats. Probably a wild dog. Let's say it is the ChupaCabra…" He pulled a pistol from his backpack. "I'm ready."

Rosa was surprised. "A gun? How did you—"

"How did I get it through security? I broke it down and stashed it with the cameras. Went right through. Listen, I grew up in the barrio. I always packed. Let's say it's just a little added protection. I wouldn't shoot the little monster. Not unless it tried to bite me!" He laughed.

"A gun is not a good idea," Rosa protested. "Mexican laws are very strict—"

"Relax, Rosa. The only shooting I'm going to do is with the camera. Hey, it's a beautiful night, I've got the equipment I need. Why waste the opportunity?"

"Let him stay if he wants," Alfredo said, "but you cannot stay, Rosa. If I go back and tell Herminio you plan to spend the night, he will come for you."

"Yes, you're right."

Herminio and Alfredo felt responsible for her. And Lupe would absolutely not allow her to spend the night in the jungle.

"It's settled," José said. "There's no sense in both of us staying. You head back with Alfredo. Look, I really doubt anything is going to show up. Maybe I'll just get photos of monkeys and iguanas. But if it's something else, then we can see it on film. That's what we came for, isn't it?"

Rosa nodded. She couldn't argue with that. "Hey, I'm staying," José insisted.

"Damn! You have a hard head!"

José smiled. "Just what my mom says."

Rosa turned to Alfredo. "Do you think we can carry the goat?"

Alfredo winced. "¿Que? Carry a dead cabrito? Rosa, you are as crazy as your friend."

"I want Herminio to look at it. Maybe he can tell us what killed it."

Alfredo shrugged. "Only for you would I do this. Help me, José."

After Alfredo and José had wrapped the kid in a tarp and tied it, Rosa turned to José. "Are you sure you're going to be all right?"

"Hey, this is a once in a lifetime opportunity. If there's something out there, I want to catch it on film. Nobody's ever done that. I *won't* miss the chance."

"Bueno," Alfredo agreed, picking up the goat and swinging it over his shoulder. "Vamos," he said to Rosa. He didn't want to be in the jungle at night. And he was not happy to be carrying a goat killed by ChupaCabra.

"Cuidate," Rosa said. She took José's hand.

"Hey, I survived the White Fence and Big Hazard gangs. This is a picnic. Go on, I'll be okay. See you in the morning."

Rosa followed Alfredo, and when they were near the village they took the road to Herminio's home.

Herminio and Lupe were sitting on the porch when they arrived. Lupe was overjoyed. She hurried to gather Rosa in an embrace. "Ay, Rosa, que gusto me da que estas con nosotros. Thank you for the regalito—"

"You're welcome, Lupe. I am glad to see you. It's been so long.

"Too long," Lupe said. "But now you are with us. I feel so happy—" She paused and looked at the goat Alfredo carried.

Rosa looked at Herminio. "I came for help."

"One of the goats ChupaCabra killed," Herminio said.

"I need to know what killed it."

"Ay, Rosa, you and your science. One day it will get you in trouble. Bueno, bring it around the back."

Alfredo carried the goat to a small shed in back of the house. Herminio lit an oil lamp and told Alfredo to place the goat on an old coconut tree stump that served as a work table.

He examined the goat carefully. "Let's see if there is any blood." He took a knife and cut the goat's throat. "No, the goat's blood was not drained."

"So what killed the goat?" Rosa asked.

"I don't know," Herminio replied, examining the goat again. "Ah, look at this."

He pointed to the top of the goat's skull.

"Looks like two holes," Rosa said, peering at the puncture wounds. "Something bore into the skull?"

Herminio nodded. He took a saw and cut into the goat's head. When he was done he pried the halves apart. The gray matter was mush.

"Dios mío!" he cried. "ChupaCabra is not drinking the blood of animals; the monster destroys their brains."

Rosa stifled a cry and felt her stomach heave. She turned away, afraid she was going to faint.

CHAPTER FOUR

Rosa sat on the porch and sipped the tea Lupe had prepared for her.

"Ay, hijita," Lupe said, holding her hand to Rosa's forehead. "Que susto. But your color is returning." She turned to Herminio. "You shouldn't have let Rosa see that awful thing."

Herminio shrugged. "She wanted a scientific experiment." He stared into the dark and brooding jungle. Something was moving out there, and it wasn't just the creatures of the jungle. Something other than the iguanas and parrots had come to the selva.

"Don't blame him," Rosa said. "He only did what I asked him to do. At least now we know how the goat died."

"But what animal would take the brains of a goat and leave the meat?" Alfredo mused.

"It is not an animal we know," Herminio whispered. All his life he had lived at the edge of the jungle. He knew the animals. Long ago the last of the jaguars had been exterminated, hunted down by the campesinos who raised goats. No, this was not an animal they knew.

"You need to rest," Lupe told Rosa.

Rosa stood. "Yes, I am tired. It's been a long day. I feel I acted like a wimp."

"Hey," Alfredo interjected. "Don't blame yourself. I almost lost my tacos." He laughed, trying to reassure Rosa.

"I'm sure there's a logical explanation," Rosa said, looking at Herminio. He didn't reply. "Anyway, I thank you for your hospitality. And for the tea, Lupe. It was just what I needed. Gracias."

"De nada," Lupe replied. "Take care of yourself. Get some rest. Tomorrow you will feel better. Come and have breakfast with us."

"Gracias," Rosa replied, embracing Lupe. "Gracias por todo."

"I'll walk you back to the hotel," Alfredo volunteered.

Exchanging buenas noches, the two departed. They walked in silence down the dirt road to the hotel.

Rosa paused at the entrance. "What do you think, Alfredo?"

"The way the goat died is unexplainable. The people here in the colonia are afraid. Some of them have moved away. That's how deep the fear goes."

"It's not right," Rosa said. "This is their land."

"Not anymore," Alfredo said sadly.

"What do you mean?"

"Remember the man called Malorio? He built a hut up there. Calls himself a brujo. He and Jefe are buddies. They came about a year ago. Started buying properties. They have bought half the mountain. When people will not sell they threaten them. Some people got sick after not selling to him. So maybe he is a brujo."

"I remember him," Rosa said. "I ran into him the last time I was here."

"I didn't know," Alfredo said. "Was it near the lago?"

"Yes. It was dark . . . he came up behind me and grabbed me."

Alfredo was surprised. "You didn't tell us."

"It was nothing. I put it out of my mind. He shouted something about the curse of the ChupaCabra."

"A curse," Alfredo said with a shiver. "The people say his curse makes people sick."

A curse, Rosa thought. Had Malorio cursed her?

"I don't believe in curses," Rosa said. "Do you?"

"I don't know what to believe. Jefe and Malorio drive to town in fancy cars. They hire some Columbianos to work for them. Malorio promises to catch the ChupaCabra and take it away. So the people bow to him. Lago Negro has changed. Well, I must go. Work tomorrow."

"Gracias por todo, Alfredo. You are very kind to take time with me."

"I am glad to help, Rosa. Like you, I want this mystery of the ChupaCabra cleared up. It isn't good for our village. I will come tomorrow evening. Buenas noches."

"Buenas noches."

"Cuidate," Alfredo said in parting. Be careful.

The hotel was dark but Rosa found her room even though the electricity was out. On the dresser she found a candle. She took a quick shower by candlelight and went to bed. Even though she was exhausted, her sleep was plagued by nightmares. All night she tossed and turned. At times she would rest, then the images of the skull Herminio had split open would reappear.

Somewhere in the nightmarish images a man dressed in monkey furs appeared—but it wasn't a man. It was a creature of the jungle, a beast with claws and sharp teeth. It descended from the sky, like a vampire, and it attacked a man. The man cried for help. He cried Rosa's name, and she recognized José.

Rosa awoke screaming, "José!" Was the dream a warning? Was José in trouble? She glanced at her watch. She dressed quickly and walked into the empty lobby. Outside a bank of ocean fog enveloped the hillside. The moisture covered the jungle like a curtain. Only a pale light illuminated the east. She glanced at her watch. Six AM.

Alfredo's gone to work and there's no need to bother Herminio, Rosa thought. Besides, it was only a bad dream.

She hurried up the path into the jungle. She was panting by the time she came to the place where they had left José. She was about to shout his name when she saw someone move under the dark canopy of trees.

She felt relieved. It's José. I worried for nothing.

"José!" she called, and the figure disappeared. An eerie silence descended on the jungle. Not even birds cried a morning greeting. Rosa spotted the hump of the dead goat.

She called his name again. "José. Where are you?"

She was about to step out of the dark shadows when she tripped. She fell hard on the damp ground, then picked herself up to see what caused her fall. She picked up José's camera and felt a chill in her blood. She knew something terrible had happened.

"José!" she called again, her heart pounding.

Then she spotted him slumped against a tree. She rushed to kneel beside him. "José," she whispered, touching his forehead. It was cold. She felt his throat; there was no pulse. Bending to get a closer look, she spied two puncture wounds on the top of his head.

"José!" she screamed over and over, her cries of terror echoing in the mist that rolled over the dark forest.

CHAPTER FIVE

By the time Rosa stumbled into Herminio's home she was muddy, her shirt and jeans torn by jungle vines. Lupe crossed her forehead. "En el nombre de Dios," she cried, gathering Rosa in her arms and helping her into the house.

Between sobs Rosa told them what had happened. "It's all my fault," she kept repeating over and over. "I should have known better."

José, one of the brightest teaching assistants in the department and an accomplished photographer, was now dead. Rosa blamed herself.

"I'll take a few men," Herminio volunteered. "Stay with Lupe."

An hour later the men arrived with José's body. Lupe had called the police and two bored policemen came to investigate. They asked perfunctory questions, and one jotted the answers down in a notebook.

"We can do nothing," they said in the end.

"But he's an American citizen!" Rosa protested.

"Señorita," one answered, "he should not be in the jungle. Tourists must stay in the tourist areas. Why was he in the selva? Maybe he is a traficante, no?"

"Of course not!" Rosa retorted.

"Okay, okay. But if I investigate further, a lot of bad things might come up. He was on private property. It is best you return home. There is nothing we can do."

They would file a report and that was the end of that.

There was no funeral home in the village, so Herminio took the body into Puerto Vallarta. Rosa would fly back home that afternoon.

"You need protection from this evil," Lupe said, taking the silver chain from around her neck and putting it on Rosa. "This cross will keep you safe."

Rosa thanked her and looked at the cross. It was an exquisite Taxco design with a small turquoise stone at the center.

"It is the eye of God," Lupe explained.

"Gracias." Rosa embraced her. "Gracias por todo."

She returned to the hotel to call José's family. By now the news of the death was known in the village. Women and children turned away when Rosa passed. They believed she was cursed by the monster from el lago, el ChupaCabra.

Rosa dreaded having to relate the bad news to José's mother. When she called an older brother answered, and Rosa talked to him. She could hear the mother's sobs in the background when she was told about José's death. The brother wanted to know every detail. When he learned José had been alone, his questions became accusations. After the difficult conversation with the brother, Rosa called the airline to make reservations for herself and arrangements to have the body flown back. She felt responsible for her friend's death. Who or what had killed José? She had to go back to the lago to find out.

In the lobby she ran into El Jefe and his crony. El Jefe grinned.

"I warned you to mind your own business, pocha. Now your friend is dead."

"Murdered!" Rosa shot back.

El Jefe sneered. "Everyone knows the ChupaCabra killed him. By this afternoon the village will be deserted. The ChupaCabra has killed a man. The people know he will come to kill again."

"I don't believe it!" Rosa countered and shoved past him.

"Believe what you want, pocha!" he shouted. "Just don't go into the jungle! You carry the curse of the ChupaCabra!"

Rosa heard his laughter mocking her. She owed it to José to go to the lago. Alfredo was working and Herminio hadn't yet returned from Puerto Vallarta, so she would go alone.

The jungle was deathly still. No birds called, no iguanas scurried along the jungle floor. Once Rosa thought she had taken the wrong path. The thick canopy of trees blocked out the light, making the way confusing.

Then she spied the clearing and smelled the stench coming from the dead goat. She skirted the clearing and found the path to the lago.

Here the jungle was even thicker, wet and dripping. Vines held moss like dead flesh, and when Rosa pushed the vines aside the slimy stuff clung to her. She was relieved to spot the small, dark lake.

She walked to the edge. The lago was only a pond, but it looked deep. The water was black. A thin mist rose from the lake, as if beneath the surface the water was boiling. The smell of sulfur touched Rosa's nostrils.

Something in the lake called to Rosa, like the song of la Llorona crying for the lost souls of her children. Was it José's spirit calling to her? Had José come here last night? Was his murderer nearby?

Come to me, the spirit voice called, and for a dizzying moment Rosa stood teetering at the edge of the dark water.

A noise startled her and she turned to see a frightening figure.

"Malorio," Rosa whispered.

"You remember me, pocha," Malorio replied. He held a staff in the shape of a winding snake.

Rosa reached for the cross at her neck and Malorio hesitated.

Rosa gathered her courage and stepped forward. "You killed José!" she accused.

Malorio glared at her. "Stupid girl! Don't you know the ChupaCabra killed your friend."

"Your ChupaCabra!" Rosa retorted.

"Yes. You remember the last time we met!"

Rosa trembled. Something terrible had happened the first time she met Malorio. He was the one who cursed her in the name of the ChupaCabra.

"It was here," she whispered.

"Yes. This is the ChupaCabra's home. Now it belongs to me!"

"Impossible," Rosa shot back.

"Oh yes, es muy posíble," he replied gruffly. "Hasn't your friend told you? I own this property. This entire mountain is mine. And you know why? Because the ChupaCabra lives here. I will trap the beast and take it to Los Angeles! It will curse everyone!"

He laughed and the grating sound echoed in the forest.

"You can't!" Rosa shouted.

"Tonta! I should drown you now and be done with you!" He stepped forward as if to strike Rosa, then hesitated. "No, that is too easy. I will let the ChupaCabra curse take care of you."

"I don't believe in curses," Rosa countered.

"Oh, you will. He is very strong; he can come and go as he desires. He will come after you."

"Let him. I have protection!" She held up her cross.

"That will not help you. ChupaCabra comes to rule the world!"

"You're insane," Rosa cried.

"Loco? No. You have seen the goats. You have seen your friend. ChupaCabra destroys the brains of those who follow him!"

"José didn't follow him!" Rosa protested and took another step forward. "You are the murderer."

She knew she could show no fear. If Malorio was going to kill her and dump her in the lake, then she was going to go down fighting.

"You carry the curse of the ChupaCabra," Malorio intoned. "Others will also die!"

"I'm not afraid of your curse!" Rosa shouted. "It has no power over me!"

"Look!" He pointed at the lake.

Rosa turned to see a shadow standing in the mist. It was José! Go back, his spirit seemed to cry. Do not seek the secret of the ChupaCabra. You will die....

Then the mist swirled savagely, and the ghost disappeared. Rosa turned, and Malorio too was gone.

Rosa trembled. Was she seeing things? Had José's spirit really returned to warn her? Filled with dread she returned to the spot where that morning she had found José's body. She picked up his belongings and returned to the hotel.

In her room she knelt by the side of the bed, made the sign of the cross, and said a silent prayer.

Later, standing under the steaming shower, she kept telling herself she didn't believe in curses. She dressed and packed her things for the long trip back to Los Angeles. As she looked up the hillside into the jungle she made a vow: "I swear I will find whoever killed José. Justice will be done."

CHAPTER SIX

José's family was waiting at the airport. They had many questions, which Rosa found difficult to answer. How did he die? Were the police in Puerto Vallarta investigating? What was he doing in the jungle? Why had she allowed him to remain alone?

Everyone was crying. José's mother was so distraught she couldn't speak. José's oldest brother was full of accusations.

"José should never have been there," he said. "You're responsible for his death."

There was nothing Rosa could say. She felt the guilt they heaped on her.

When she finally parted from them, she felt drained. She loaded her equipment into her car and rode home in a daze. Mechanically she called the department secretary at the university and told her about José's death. Then she called Tomás at Self-Help and explained what had happened.

Finally she called Eddie. He had graduated with a degree in theater and was directing at Centro de la Raza. Rosa had taken the kids she was tutoring to a Cherie Moraga play, and Eddie had invited them backstage after the performance. He was great with the kids.

After that she attended all his productions, and a close, platonic friendship developed. Rosa's interest in Chicana literature and Eddie's love of theater drew them together. Rosa confessed she had often thought of writing a play, something based on la Llorona's tragic life.

"ChupaCabra meets la Llorona. I love it!" Eddie had cried. "I'll direct it."

But both were involved in their own demanding careers, so their relationship consisted of phone calls or an occasional concert. If Santana was in town, they would be there.

Rosa briefly explained what had happened, and he said he would be right over. When she opened the door he gathered her in his arms.

"Eddie, I'm so glad to see you—"

"Rosa, thank God you're safe. Ay, mihita, I can't believe what you've been through. Sit down, tell me what happened."

Rosa told him everything as she made coffee. Talking helped, and Eddie was a good listener. They sat in her small kitchen and she finished relating the events that had cost José his life.

"I'm feeling so guilty," she said at the end.

"It wasn't your fault," Eddie insisted. "Things happen. Things happen on the street every day. The good get caught in the crossfire and die."

"God's mysterious ways " Rosa nodded, fingering the cross at her throat. Malorio had hesitated when he saw the cross. Could it really protect her?

"So you think it was the ChupaCabra?" Eddie asked.

"I don't know what to believe," Rosa replied. "Something or someone killed him. It was no accident."

"I always thought the ChupaCabra was a fantasy. Like the boogeyman—the Coco Man, el Cucúi. Some monster in the dark would get us if we misbehaved. Don't be a malcriado, my parents said. Get home on time. They frightened me to make sure I didn't get in trouble. Today the kids don't believe in those scary stories. Try telling the homeboys they better quit the gang or la Llorona will get them and they laugh at you."

"Is our cultura changing that much?" Rosa mused.

"It is on the street. The new culture is street culture. For the homies the ChupaCabra is just one more dope dealer. Their reality is the man who has power on the streets. Money, big car, mota, booze, meth."

"You're a realist, Eddie."

"Hey, I grew up in East Los. I had to be a realist to survive. Primero Flats and Maravilla are nothing compared to the gangs out there now."

"I have so much to learn," Rosa whispered.

From high school in Santa Fe she had gone straight to college. She had been protected along the way. It was time to get tough. For José.

"How do we explain the way he died?"

"I don't know," Eddie said.

That was the scary part. There was no logical explanation.

"How did you get started investigating the ChupaCabra?"

"I was visiting my parents in Santa Fe. One of my cousins has a ranch near Mora. That's up in the mountains. One of his bulls had been mutilated. I went to see it. Only the private parts had been cut away. No meat was taken, just the private parts cut out with surgical precision. There were no tracks at the scene."

"Could have been coyotes," Eddie suggested.

"Coyotes and mountain lions will eat the carcass. No, this was something that puzzled the ranchers. The year before one man found strange burn marks near a mutilated cow. Aliens in UFOs, the people said."

"Green men from Mars, huh." Eddie smiled.

"Something like that. Then I started reading the reports from Puerto Rico. Animals found dead, drained of their blood.

Reports from Mexico. Last year a report came from Lago Negro, so I flew down there. That's when I met Alfredo, and Herminio and his wife. I had no idea it would escalate to this."

"Do you think those cattle mutilations in New Mexico are related to what happened in Puerto Rico and Mexico?"

"I don't know."

"Is there any pattern to the reports?"

"Only that they're spreading. There have been reports here in California. One near Calexico. One in South Chicago. And they seem to be getting more violent. And now—"

Eddie took her hand. "Look, you need some rest. You look pale. Have you eaten?"

Rosa shook her head. She hadn't eaten all day.

"I'll warm you some sopa, and then you have to get to bed."

"Gracias. Thanks for listening."

"It helps to talk. I've got kids coming in to rehearse." He paused. "Are you afraid to stay alone?"

"No. It's just the nightmare—"

"You're still having the same nightmare?"

"Yes."

"Do you think the nightmares come to warn you?"

"I should have listened. I shouldn't have gone to Lago Negro. Then José would still be alive—"

"Listen, Rosa, quit blaming yourself. Maybe you should go to the police."

"What can they do?"

"Call the police in Puerto Vallarta. See if they've found any new information. Maybe they picked up Malorio."

Rosa shook her head. "They won't do a damn thing. They have no reason to interview Malorio."

"Does he control ChupaCabra?"

"He says he does. But I think ChupaCabra is something bigger. He can be anywhere." She shivered.

"Yeah, well if he comes to East L.A. the homeboys are going to kick his ass."

Rosa had to smile. Eddie was helpful, a friend she could trust, but she realized she hadn't told him about Malorio's curse. That dark bothersome secret that she couldn't express.

"Come on, I'm going to fix you a bite, then it's bed and rest for you."

Rosa showered and got into bed while Eddie prepared her something to eat. "Soup and crackers," he said when he entered the bedroom with a tray. "My specialty."

"Thanks, Eddie, thanks for being such a good friend."

"What are friends for? Get some rest."

"You're wonderful. Thanks."

"Call me if you need anything." He kissed her, then waved goodbye.

"Break a leg," she whispered as she heard him close the front door. She turned on some music and ate the noodle soup. Not feeling like tackling the research paper she was writing, she reached for the book she was reading. A murder mystery by Lucha Corpi.

So many new Chicana writers, she thought. Each one has so much to offer. I have to concentrate on my work. Get my dissertation published.

She knew she wasn't going to get any work done during spring break. She worried. There was a lot of pressure for her to publish if she was going to keep her job. And her parents had expected her home. She hadn't even had time to call them.

Her thoughts were on José. Why did he have to die? Why in such a cruel way? He was so young and full of promise, then he was gone. He had been eager to learn about the mysterious ChupaCabra, and it cost him his life. Will it cost me mine? thought Rosa.

She fell into a troubled sleep. The nightmare came and plunged her into a miasma of terror. She found herself in a dark forest, behind her she heard the footsteps of a monster. She screamed and ran, but there was no escape.

She bolted awake, gasping for breath. She looked around her room to get her bearings. She was home, safe, not in the jungle. Then the fatigue of the journey and her sadness dragged her back down into a troubled sleep.

The monster reappeared, fanning its wings, rising above her as she ran. Blood dripping from its fangs, it closed in on her. She ran, crashing through the forest, feeling the stinging whips of branches, her body slashed and bleeding, her blood exciting the monster, which suddenly blocked her escape.

She recognized the face.

"Malorio!" she screamed and awakened.

The phone was ringing. Rosa glanced at her watch. She had slept late.

"Hello."

"Rosa, it's me, Eddie. Have you seen the paper?"

"No, I slept late—"

"I figured you would, that's why I didn't call earlier. José's death is spread all over the L.A. *Times*. Page one. *Mysterious Mexican Monster Kills Young Ph.D. Student*. That's the lead. It's got your picture in it."

"Oh, God, no," Rosa whispered.

CHAPTER SEVEN

The phone continued to ring, but Rosa didn't answer it. Without caller ID she couldn't tell who was calling, and Eddie had warned her that reporters would be after her like a pack of pit bulls. To be chased by the paparazzi was a dubious honor.

She started her aerobic exercises, but she was still tired. Her morning jog was out of the question. After coffee and pan dulce she picked up her guitar and strummed. Holding the guitar took her back to the time she and her father had played at the Santa Fe Fiesta. They had taken first prize in the amateur contest. Those were good times, she thought, family times.

Taking a deep breath, she called her parents and explained as much as she dared. She heard worry in their voices. She should come home right away, get away from the tragedy. She needed the rest. She listened with gratitude, they were concerned for her, but no, there was too much to do, she said in the end. A trip home would have to wait.

Later in the afternoon she headed for Self-Help Graphics. She couldn't stay home feeling depressed. She had to go about her business, which meant dealing with reality. She would attend her regularly scheduled meeting with the kids she tutored.

The receptionist came around the desk and embraced her. "I'm sorry, Rosa. What a terrible thing!" She pointed at the newspaper lying on her desk. "Are you all right? You don't have to meet the kids today—"

"Thank you, Consuelo, but it's best I tell them what happened. Are they here?"

"All except Chuco. Tomás is out looking for him . . ."

Rosa sighed. Looking for Chuco meant he probably had dropped out of the program and was back on the street.

"Let me know if he finds him," she said and hurried to a classroom in the back. Indio, Mousey, and Leo were waiting for her.

"Hey, teach, heard you were in the news," Indio said.

"Cool, profe!" Leo exclaimed, getting up to put her arm around Rosa. "You were in Mexico and somebody got killed by the ChupaCabra. Que loco. Que pasó? Tell us."

"It's in the paper," Mousey added. "The ChupaCabra's all over. How did you do it?"

"I'll explain everything later. Where's Chuco?" Rosa replied.

"Ah, you know Chuco," Mousey said. "He's checking out the homies."

"Homies or drogas?" Rosa questioned and turned to Leo. "Leonora?"

"Probably got a job." Leo shrugged. "His father works for city parks. Maybe he got hired."

"Damn!" Rosa exclaimed. She slammed her books on the table. "You know damn well he hasn't gotten a job! He's out scoring, isn't he!"

Mousey nodded. "You know Chuco—"

"No I don't!" Rosa replied. "I guess I don't know any of you. I work with you for months and I don't know you. Why don't you talk to us when you get in trouble? Talk to me or Tomás, or one of the counselors. You don't because it's easier to fall back. Go score some meth! Screw the world that's trying to help you. Is that what you think?"

She realized she had been shouting, and the three were looking up at her with blank expressions. That's what a lecture always drew. Lectures didn't work with these kids. They were too tough; they had lived on the mean streets too long.

Rosa knew that. She sat and leaned her head in her hands. She didn't want to cry.

Please God, make me strong. I don't want to cry.

"You okay, profe?" Leo asked, touching her shoulder.

Rosa looked up. "Yeah, I'm okay."

"Get her a drink of water," Leo said to Mousey, who jumped up and ran out of the room.

"Chuco was having a tough time," Leo explained. "The vatos from his old gang didn't want to let him go. You can't leave the gang. They got to him. So maybe he went back."

Rosa knew. Life on the streets was a dead-end game. And Chuco had tried hard, but the homies kept calling him back. The gang provided a measure of safety and belonging; the gang was the adopted family. What could she, a young assistant professor trying to be a good teacher, offer?

Indio, who had been silent, spoke. "Hey, Chuco can handle it. He's tough."

Rosa nodded. Yeah, tough. They were just kids, in their late teens, and already they had experienced life at its worst. They had to be tough to survive.

Rosa sipped the water Mousey offered. "Just for once I'd like to meet someone who says they're soft. Not tough."

The three looked at each other.

Mousey replied. "Hey, if you're soft out there you get eaten alive. No, teach, we gotta be tough. Even a mouse like me has to be tough, or I get eaten by the big, bad gato."

They laughed. They understood the rules of the game.

"Maybe you can teach us to be like you," Leo whispered.

"Sure," Rosa patted her hand. "And you teach me to be muy fuerte."

"You're tough," Indio said. "I read in the paper you and José were chasing the ChupaCabra."

He acts like he doesn't give a damn about the world, but he reads the paper, Rosa thought, looking at Indio. Good.

"The ChupaCabra!" Mousey exclaimed. "Wow, you don't want to mess with him!"

"Is that really what you were doing?" Leo asked.

They gathered around her and Rosa told them the story. They wanted to know every detail, and especially why she was so interested in the monster everybody called the ChupaCabra. They remembered José and were saddened by his death.

When she was done, they looked at her with new respect. They thought she only knew books, but she had been out in the Mexican jungle chasing a monster. She had lost a friend, like they had lost friends on the streets. So, the professor from Cal State *was* tough.

"You've been through a lot," Leo said. "Why did you come today? Why not just take the day off?"

"I guess I came because I need you," Rosa confessed. The kids she tutored had become her gang. She could speak to them like she couldn't to any of her colleagues in the department. There a person was judged on the number of articles or books published, and most conversations revolved around academics.

Here she had an emotional investment. She belonged to the kids, and they belonged to her.

The three looked at her in silence. Few had ever told them they were needed. Rosa did. She needed them. They never thought of their relationships that way. She was the tutor who helped them, and that was it. Now she was someone different, a real person who had lost a friend, like they had lost friends to drugs, drive-by shootings, AIDS, and all the other dangers.

"It's tough to lose a friend," Indio said, "especially like that."

"We'll stand by you, profe," Leo added. "Whatever."

Consuelo interrupted them. She stood at the door, trembling. Her color was ashen.

"Professor Medina," she whispered.

"What is it, Consuelo?"

"Tomás just called. He found Chuco...at the crack house." Her voice quivered. "He's dead," she whispered, and burst into tears.

CHAPTER EIGHT

Rosa packed Indio, Mousey, and Leo into her Honda and they drove to the address just off Whittier. They drove in silence. The news of Chuco's death had hit them hard.

Each thought about what they might have done differently to help Chuco. Handsome, bright, and talented, he was the one they thought could succeed, if only he had been able to leave the world of gangs and drugs.

Did I fail him? Rosa thought. Was there something missing in the communication? The kids needed not only reading and writing skills, they needed to feel they belonged.

I should have worked with him, instead I went off chasing ChupaCabra. And that had gotten José killed. A wave of guilt swept over her. Within minutes they were pulling up in front of a dilapidated two-story house cordoned by police crime-scene tape. Rosa shivered. She had seen the house before, but where? Was it the house in her nightmares? The house of ChupaCabra?

"A spooky place," Leo whispered.

Behind the house lay a mechanic's garage. A couple of shadowy figures moved around among the hulks of dismembered cars. Car theft was big business, so chop shops sprang up in almost every neighborhood. Car theft and dope went hand-in-hand.

"The house is haunted," Indio volunteered.

Rosa looked at him. She knew very little about Indio. He was Navajo from New Mexico, had gotten into drugs, then left the reservation for L.A. He went clean and enrolled at Self-Help. She knew Navajos would not enter the house where a person had died. The traditional Navajos burned the hogan of the dead person.

Indio was right. The large house sitting back from the street looked haunted. Perhaps Chuco's restless spirit already wandered in the empty rooms, as did other ghosts. A lot of young men and women had sold their souls for a rush of crack or meth in this foreboding place.

"There's Tomás!" Leo pointed. Tomás, the director of Self-Help, was a veterano who would do anything for his kids.

They got out and hurried to him.

"I lost him," Tomás said, his voice quivered.

Rosa embraced him. Chuco dying really meant he had lost one of his own.

"Lo siento," Rosa said, feeling the words weren't enough to convey her sympathy, and her own sense of loss.

L.A. in the spring could be beautiful. Fresh winds came in from the ocean and swept away the smog. But today the pollution hung heavy over East L.A., and the sultry air felt sticky on the body. On days like this L.A. could also be full of murder and mayhem. Full of dead kids on the streets.

Rosa looked at the house and shivered. Chuco's spirit was calling her.

"What can I do?" Rosa asked.

Tomás shook his head. "Cops are taking care of things."

"Did you see him?"

"Yeah, I know the officer who called me. They're waiting for the medical investigator now. He took a big hit. The pipe was still clutched in his hand when they found him. Fingers burned."

Indio glanced at Rosa but said nothing.

"Can I see him?"

Her question surprised them.

"You don't want to see him, Rosa. It's not pretty. It's dirty. Sonsofbitches who deal in this stuff deal in dirt."

"It's important," Rosa said.

"Are you sure?" Tomás studied her. Her eyes told him she had to see Chuco. "Okay, I'll see what the cops say."

Indio touched Rosa's arm. She turned to face him. "You shouldn't go in there. You'll get the curse that killed Chuco."

I'm already cursed, Rosa thought. First José, then Chuco. Malorio's threat was hanging in the hot, sticky air.

"Yenaaloshi," he whispered. "A man who walks on four legs has been here."

"Yenaaloshi," Rosa repeated. Men or women who walked on four legs were called Skinwalkers in the Navajo tradition. They were witches. The yenaaloshi covered himself in the skin of a wolf and walked on four legs.

The Spanish-speaking people of New Mexico knew about witches. Rosa had heard many stories about witches who took the shape of owls or coyotes when they went to do evil. Near one of the pueblos a witch had taken the form of a burro. Some witches traveled as balls of fire across the countryside. And there were stories about people who had been cursed by a witch. But the Navajo considered it taboo to speak of anything that had to do with witchcraft. Was Indio warning her? Was the house cursed?

"Who saw the man that walks like a wolf?" she asked. Indio's vacant stare told her he had seen it.

"There aren't any Skinwalkers in L.A.," Rosa managed feebly. But the minute she said that, she realized her mistake. Wherever people went they took their stories and beliefs with them. And witchcraft was a deeply held belief among some Navajo.

"Can we go with you?" Leo interrupted.

"Not me," Mousey chimed in, shaking his head. "I'm with Indio. I'll see Chuco at the funeral home."

Leo slapped his arm. "Shut up, Mousey. I'll go with you," she said to Rosa.

"No, you stay put," Rosa replied.

Tomás returned with the policeman.

"This is officer Malatesta. He'll take you in."

"Only for a look," the cop said in a very serious tone. "I understand you're a family member. Okay, as long as we're waiting for the crime lab, you can have a look. Ain't pretty."

He lifted the yellow tape. Rosa stepped through and followed him up the walk and into the dark living room.

"This is the office of the drug pushers. Not pretty is it? But they make a lot of money. No overhead, just a place where crack heads come to get their fix. Why they do it beats me."

Rosa glanced around the large room. Used syringes littered the floor. A large painting leaned against a wall. It was obvious someone had taken the painting from above the fireplace and leaned it on the wall. The face was that of an old man. His mouth was twisted in scorn, but it was the eyes that startled Rosa. They seemed alive and they were watching her.

"The painting," she muttered.

The officer paused. "Junk's scattered all over the house. Maybe the owner. Fifty years ago it took money to build a big place like this, now it's just a nuisance. Follow me."

He led Rosa down a hallway to a dark back room. On the floor lay a crumpled figure. Chuco. A stench hung in the air. The rush of crack that had stopped his heart had also made him soil himself.

Tomás had said it wasn't pretty. Rosa cringed. She was tempted to turn away. What was she doing here? The drug world of suffering, pain, and death wasn't her world. She was mixing in something she didn't understand.

Still, she leaned over the body and said a silent prayer. She lifted the crucifix that hung around her neck and kissed it. She looked at Chuco's face. The chiseled face of an Aztec warrior, once fiercely dark and handsome, now shriveled. He had died a painful death.

Rosa ran her fingers through his dark curly hair. She gasped when she felt dried blood. She looked closely. There was a slash across the scalp. The mark of the ChupaCabra!

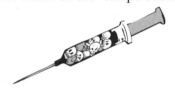

CHAPTER NINE

Rosa stumbled through the dark hallway, a cry choking her throat. She found her way to the front door and stumbled out into the arms of Tomás.

"Oh God," she cried.

"I'm sorry you had to see him like that," Tomás whispered.

Indio, Mousey, and Leo stood silent.

"You okay, lady?" the officer asked. He had followed her outside. "I told Mr. Benavídez to warn you."

"I'm okay," Rosa replied. Then she added, "The ChupaCabra killed him—"

Tomás looked puzzled. He wasn't sure he had heard her correctly. "Crack," he said.

"No!" Rosa insisted. "It was the ChupaCabra."

"It's not possible," Tomás stuttered.

"It is!"

"You sure?" Leo asked, reaching out to hold Rosa.

"Yes!"

"Chingao," Mousey cursed.

Rosa realized they were looking at her strangely. Either Rosa was just distraught from seeing Chuco dead, or people around her were being killed by ChupaCabra.

"I don't understand," Tomás said.

"The curse of the ChupaCabra," Rosa said. Now she was sure. She was cursed, and anyone she touched was equally cursed. "Don't you see, it's not only in Mexico. It can be everywhere!"

She looked at Indio and he nodded. For him ChupaCabra was a Skinwalker, an evil witch. And yes, they, like ChupaCabra, could be everywhere.

"You better get home...rest," Tomás said, taking her arm.

"Can you drive them back to the Center?" Rosa asked.

"Sure, but are you going to be all right? You should come with us—"

"Can't," Rosa said, turning and hurrying to her car. She had to get away. She had to think the whole thing through. Had she really seen the mark of the ChupaCabra? Was she experiencing panic because of the two deaths? And the curse? Did she really believe it?

She drove aimlessly until she spotted a bar she recognized. She had been there once, at a book party for Nina Martínez. She drove into the lot and parked. She needed help, someone to talk to. But she didn't want to frighten her parents. If her father knew what had happened he would be on the next plane to L.A.

Eddie? She called him on her cell phone, and he said he could be at the bar in a few minutes.

She went inside, found a booth, and took out her compact. A pale face stared back at her. Her fingers trembled as she touched lipstick to her lips.

She didn't want to believe in Malorio's curse, but how else could she explain the death of two people close to her? Death by the monster that destroyed brains. It wasn't a coincidence. The monster from Lago Negro was now stalking its prey in East L.A.

"What would you like to drink?" the waitress asked.

"Coffee, please," Rosa managed.

"Coffee it is." The waitress paused. "You okay?"

"Yes, why?"

"You look a little pale, that's all. Coffee coming right up."

"Thanks for asking. I'm fine. I've got a friend coming."

"Good," the waitress replied. "You need anything, just call."

Rosa was sipping her coffee when Eddie rushed in. She waved.

"Rosa, what happened? Your voice—" He slid into the booth and took her hands in his.

She explained what had happened to Chuco and finished by saying, "I've been sitting here trying to come up with a logical explanation."

"Rosa, Chuco wasn't your fault. He made a bad choice—"

"But I'm the link. I brought the curse. Don't you see—"

"Hey," Eddie interrupted. "You've been through a lot. And you're still blaming yourself. There is no curse. This is one time we have to trust the cops. Let them investigate what happened."

"How will they explain what I saw?"

"There has to be an explanation. It has nothing to do with a curse. He overdosed, probably fell and hit his head. That explains it."

Rosa sighed. "So the ChupaCabra is just a story. But do stories become real?"

"People love a good story," Eddie said. "We Latinos are good at it. But stories aren't real."

"Isn't la Llorona real?" Rosa asked. "Mothers do kill their children. La Llorona's story becomes real."

"Yes, young women kill their children. Because of postpartum depression. Or the husband is running around, or abusive. La Llorona's story just tells us those things can happen."

"Her stories frighten us...."

"Yeah, but just while the story is told. I mean, you don't get real susto from a story."

"Susto. I wonder if that's what I'm feeling."

44

"Yes," Eddie said. "Two people in your life have died. That's traumatic. Your nervous system is in shock. I remember when I was a kid and fell off my bike. Going to the hospital scared the hell out of me. I couldn't sleep. My mom took me to a healer, a curandera."

"I need a curandera." Rosa smiled weakly.

"Yes. And lots of rest," Eddie replied.

"Am I hallucinating?"

"Nah. You're too smart for that. You need rest. That's all."

"You're right. I should visit my amiga, la curandera. But I don't have time. I have to find—"

"ChupaCabra?"

"Yes."

Eddie shook his head. "Look, creatures like ChupaCabra were okay when we were primitives living in the jungle. Our ancestors in the cave saw monsters in the night; they told stories about the monsters they imagined."

"We still have monsters in our nights," Rosa said.

"Yeah, you got a point there. There are monsters in the city. The urban jungle. Rage, violence, drugs. Maybe you should talk to the cops."

"Why?"

"You're in danger."

Rosa stared at him. She hadn't thought of herself in danger, but if ChupaCabra was stalking the streets, then the curse of Malorio could strike her next.

CHAPTER TEN

Eddie knew a detective in LAPD who might help them. He called Bobby Mejía and asked him who was handling José's death.

"What's your role in this?" Bobby wanted to know.

"I'm trying to help Rosa," Eddie explained.

Reluctantly Bobby gave him the name: Detective Frank Dill. Then he added, "I wouldn't get involved if I were you. And don't mention to anyone you talked to me. You got that?"

"Yeah, sure," Eddie replied.

He snapped his cell phone shut and looked at Rosa. "Bobby's a cool vato, but he's barely cooperating. Anyway, I'm going to call the man and insist he tell us what he knows."

Eddie called Detective Dill, who at first refused to see them. When Eddie said he would go straight to the division captain, Dill gave in.

Rosa followed Eddie to First Street and Chicago, the Hollenbeck Division in Boyle Heights. She parked beside him and they went inside. A secretary pointed to the cubicle where a heavy-set, crew-cut man sat hunched over his desk, working on a crossword puzzle.

Rosa and Eddie approached the detective's desk. Rosa coughed softly.

"Mr. Dill?"

The man looked up. His steel blue eyes took Rosa in. His face was puffy, red. He was muscular, like a construction worker, not anything like the detectives on TV. Certainly not like Jimmy Smits on *NYPD Blue*. He wore an old-fashioned shoulder holster.

"I'm detective Frank Dill. What do you need?"

"I'm Dr. Rosa Medina. This is Eddie López. We just called—"

"Oh, yeah." He pointed to chairs. "Yeah. Sit down. You called about the man who died in Mexico. Splashed all over the paper."

Rosa nodded.

"You're the woman who was with him. The doctor?"

"I'm not a medical doctor. Ph.D. in literature."

"I see. Well even if you were a medical doctor, you couldn't have done much. Autopsy just came in. His brains were fried."

"Can you be more exact?" Eddie asked.

"Cooked," Dill said.

"Don't you find that strange?" asked Rosa.

Dill laughed. "Not really. Your homeboys use crack. It burns their brains. Meth does the same. So does sniffing paint. After a while you see them wandering on the streets. Till they drop."

Rosa felt they weren't getting anywhere. "We just came from a murder scene. One of my students was found dead."

"Name?"

"Valentín Guerrero."

"Where?"

"A crack house over on Mott Street."

Dill nodded. "One of your students, huh?" His eyes bored into her, and Rosa shivered. She would hate to be interrogated by this man. He was large and threatening. There wasn't a soft edge to him. "So that makes two men connected to you who are dead."

"What do you mean *connected*?" Eddie said, his voice rising.

"They were her students, and—let me ask you. This guy Valentín, that wouldn't be Chuco Guerrero would it?"

"Yes."

"We've got a file on him. Belonged to Primero Flats. So he bought the farm, huh? Both he and the boy who died in Mexico were crackheads—"

"José wasn't a crackhead!" Rosa exploded. "He never did drugs. I know Chuco had been in the gang, but José was working on a Ph.D. in literature. He was my teaching assistant."

"Oh, he was into drugs all right," Dill replied. "I dug up his file when the family came demanding the police do something about his death. He was busted when he was in high school. Arrested very near where this Chuco boy was found dead."

"Are you sure it's the same José?" Eddie asked.

"I double checked," Dill said. "Maybe José went clean, but I doubt it. Once they taste crack or meth, they're hooked."

Rosa shook her head. José had never spoken of his past. He was a talented graduate student, a genius she thought. He was an excellent photographer, and he got along so well with both professors and fellow students. Nothing suggested he had ever done drugs. But she knew very little about his past.

"Maybe it was a mistake," Rosa said. "He was at the wrong place, wrong time..."

"Innocent victim syndrome, huh? Same old excuse. He was into crack, all right. Made a deal to go to detox. But I don't think any of those guys ever stay clean."

"He was clean!" Rosa shot back. "I worked with him every day. He was *not* doing drugs!"

Dill shrugged, as if to say *believe what you want, lady.*

"It doesn't matter if he took drugs when he was in high school," Eddie cut in. "The question is, what have you found out from the Mexican police?"

"Nothing," Dill answered.

"What do you mean nothing?" Rosa asked.

"We're not trying very hard, lady," Dill replied. He got up and poured himself a cup of coffee.

"Why aren't you trying?" Eddie asked.

Dill turned to face them. "He was killed in Mexico. Has nothing to do with us."

"Nothing to do with you ..." Rosa repeated. "What do you mean?"

"They gave me the case because the family came to complain to the Chief. But near as I can tell there's no federal offense. So even the FBI won't get into it. It's up to the Mexican police."

"But now you have a similar murder here," Eddie said.

"According to you," Dill answered, sipping his coffee. "I'll check into the report."

"José died a mysterious death. Don't you have to investigate the circumstances?"

Dill smiled. "Ah, I see what you're getting at. The ChupaCabra, huh? I read the papers. Mexicans believe in that shit. Look, I'm not going to go off chasing a boogeyman. Vampires who suck blood. Your people love those stories—"

"My people!" Rosa exclaimed and stood. "You're *just* not interested, are you?"

"Like I said, professor, I'll look at the officer's report on Chuco. Take it from there."

Eddie also stood. "Look," he said sternly. "Two young men associated with Rosa have been killed under very strange circumstances. I don't care what you attribute it to. I'm concerned for Rosa. She should have police protection."

"Has anyone made threats on your life?" Dill asked.

"No—"

"I can't assign police protection unless you've been threatened."

"Two men have been killed! And you can't give her protection?" Eddie protested.

"Look!" Dill replied loudly. "If I gave protection to every person involved in a barrio drug deal, I'd be babysitting half of East L.A. This guy Chuco died in a crack house, and I'm supposed to protect you?" He looked at Rosa and shook his head.

"Don't bother," Rosa replied. "I can take care of myself. We'll find out who killed Chuco."

Dill's lack of interest had angered her at first. Then she realized that she needed to turn the anger into resolve. She had to find who or what killed José and Chuco. If the police helped, fine, if they didn't then she swore she would find the murderers. And she had to find the ChupaCabra before it struck again.

"Just don't go playing detective," Dill warned her. "That's our job."

"Looks like you're more interested in crossword puzzles than in doing your job," Rosa replied. "Come on, Eddie, let's get some fresh air."

She took Eddie's arm and together they walked out into the hazy L.A. afternoon.

CHAPTER ELEVEN

The following morning Eddie picked up Rosa, Mousey, Indio, and Leo at Self-Help. The kids wanted to attend José's funeral. Weeks ago he had taught a workshop on photography. He had taken them into the barrio, where they photographed street scenes. He had a talent for capturing the vibrancy of life in the neighborhood. He made them feel proud of their community.

"Feels strange," Leo said, "today is José's funeral and tomorrow Chuco's."

The others nodded. The sudden and horrible events had left them contemplative. In the meantime the autopsy on Chuco had been completed, and once the media found out he had died of causes similar to whatever had killed José, they had splashed it on the front pages and the evening news. A ChupaCabra sensation gripped L.A.

"A newspaper reporter called this morning," Rosa said. "He asked about Chuco's drug use. They didn't want to know the real Chuco, only about drugs. I hung up."

"Good," Eddie agreed. "Best thing is not to talk to anyone."

"He was a wizard at math," Mousey offered.

"And he was trying to get out of the gang," Leo added. "But the gang wouldn't let him out."

"Maybe the gang killed him," Mousey said.

"Drugs killed him," Rosa replied. "And a curse."

She looked at Indio. He shrugged and turned away. She knew he would not talk about Skinwalkers.

"I don't believe in brujas," Leo said. "When somebody gets sick in my family my abuela says it's witchcraft. Lo embrujaron. Or he got the mal ojo. She's so old fashioned."

"Yeah, but how do you explain the fact the brains were mush?" Mousy asked.

"Those are just words the TV reporters use," Eddie interjected. "They like to make things sensational."

"Yeah, but José died looking for the ChupaCabra in Mexico?"

Yes, Rosa thought, we were looking for ChupaCabra. Did we find it?

Last night she had been haunted by the nightmare again. She saw the house where Chuco died, the large, faded painting leaning on the wall. The eyes seemed to glare at her. There was something evil stalking her and she believed it was ChupaCabra, whatever form it took.

"We don't have answers," was all Rosa could say. "Part of the answers to the mystery are at Lago Negro, part in the crack house where Chuco died. Who owns the house?"

For a moment there was only silence, then Indio spoke. "I don't know his name but Chuco called him el Hombre Malo. Those who were dealing with him just called him Malo."

"Malo!" Rosa exclaimed. No, it couldn't be the man from Lago Negro. Impossible. "Do you know him? I mean, have you ever met him?"

"No," Indio replied. "I never did crack."

"So how did you know about the place?"

"I went with a friend."

Rosa looked at Mousey and Leo, and they shook their heads. "Do the cops know about Malo?"

"Yeah, they know," Mousey volunteered. "But they never busted him."

"Why?"

"Maybe he has connections," Leo volunteered. Indio and Mousey nodded in silent agreement.

The Resurrection cemetery came into view and Eddie pulled up. José's family and friends were already gathered around at the gravesite. Rosa hesitated. She knew José's family blamed her for his death. She wasn't sure she would be welcome at his funeral.

Eddie opened the door and took her hand. "It's okay," he whispered.

They joined the mourners in the bright spring day. The priest prayed, then blessed the coffin with holy water and incense. When he was done, the family members stepped forward to place roses on the coffin.

The family filed by the coffin, the women wiping their eyes. José's mother, sobbing for her son, paused to place a crucifix on the coffin.

Her cries tore through Rosa's heart. Am I to blame? she kept asking herself.

When the family was done the mourners were asked to step forward. Rosa held back. She loved José, for his friendship and his genius, but she couldn't bring herself to stand by his grave. She would come later, alone, and bring flowers. Then perhaps the grief she felt would find some relief.

"Vaya con Dios," she whispered. "I swear I will find those who murdered you."

With the burial ceremony concluded, the family was ushered toward the waiting limousines to return to the mother's home. All the mourners were invited to share a few hours with the family.

José's mother spotted Rosa. A few times José had invited Rosa to his mother's home for dinner. Rosa liked the woman, but now she dreaded meeting her. Her oldest son accompanied her.

The woman lifted her dark veil and said, "Rosa. How are you?" Her face was drawn with grief.

"I'm doing okay, Mrs. Bustos, but I can't tell you how sorry I am—"

"I know, Rosa, I know. José spoke of you so many times. Sometimes I thought he was in love with you. He admired you so much. Just think, mamá, he would tell me. Finally we get a Chicana professor. Finally, after all these years. And I get to be her graduate assistant. He was in heaven."

"He was gifted, Mrs. Bustos. And—"

"And now this," She nodded. "We don't know when death will come. We can only trust to God's will." She looked at her stern son standing beside her and shook her head. "José was with you when he died, Rosa. But we don't blame you."

Rosa sighed a sigh of relief. "Thank you. That means a great deal to me."

"My son did not deserve to die," she whispered. "Please promise me you will find those who murdered him."

"I will Mrs. Bustos, I will," Rosa replied.

The woman kissed Rosa's cheek. "Thank you, Rosa. Come and visit me when you have time."

She took her son's arm and Rosa watched as they made their way to the waiting limousine.

CHAPTER TWELVE

Eddie drove them back to Self-Help. The Carlos Morton play he was directing would open in a few days, and he was consumed with details.

"Don't forget, we have a date," he called as he drove away. "You're going to love the play."

"We'll be there! Thanks, Eddie!"

"What now?" Leo asked. She sensed Rosa was up to something.

"I need to know more about Malo. The man who pushes crack." She looked at Indio.

"You don't want to go near him," Indio said.

"Why?"

"Drug dealers don't like publicity," Mousey offered.

"Someone gave Chuco the drugs that killed him. I need to know who."

"Let the cops take care of it," Indio said.

"They're going to say he ODed. Case closed," Leo said, glancing at Indio and Mousey. That's the way the cops dealt with death in the barrio: chalk it off. Now their teacher knew. She was learning fast.

"So what are you going to do?" Leo asked.

"Go to the crack house, tonight."

"You're crazy!" Mousey exclaimed, then apologized. "Sorry, I mean—"

"I may be crazy, but it's something I have to do."

"He means it's dangerous," Leo said.

"I'm going," Rosa replied, and her tone told them she meant it.

"You can't go alone. I'll go with you," Leo volunteered.

Rosa shook her head. "Thanks, Leo, but like you said, it may be dangerous."

"I don't care. You can't go alone. Mousey, do something!"

Mousey looked exasperated. "Okay, okay, you need a man with you. I'll go. But I'll stay in the car."

"Thanks, Mousey, you're really brave." She pinched his cheek. She turned to Indio.

Indio shook his head. "Skinwalker," he whispered.

"Please, Indio. We can't let the teach go alone."

"You don't have to go," Rosa said. Indio had mentioned the Skinwalkers once before, and she knew he feared anything having to do with witchcraft.

But he relented. "Okay, I'll go."

"All right!" Leo gave him a high five. "Real machos, huh profe?" Leo beamed.

"I can't let you," Rosa protested. She didn't want them in harm's way.

"It's a done deal, maestra. We're not letting you go alone," Leo replied. "Besides, it's safer if we all go together."

"She's right," Mousey agreed.

"So we all go," Rosa smiled. "Meet you here at nine."

Rosa went home to an answering machine full of messages from reporters. Everybody wanted to talk to her about the

ChupaCabra deaths. The *National Enquirer* promised to pay for a story. The writer already had an angle. ChupaCabra was an alien from outer space, and the brain of the dead man had been taken for experiments. The aliens planned to develop a virus that would shrink all the brains on Earth, thus making the takeover of the planet a cinch.

Rosa cringed at the reporter's suggestion. She knew the ChupaCabra story would be blown into the wildest fantasies. A horror movie in which ChupaCabra kidnapped Latina virgins was just around the corner.

"No, thanks," Rosa said as she erased the messages. She didn't want anything to do with reporters, especially those looking only for sensational stories.

Through Tomás she was able to locate Chuco's sister. Rosa called her and found out the sister had no money for a funeral. Chuco's parents were deceased and the sister was broke. She had turned the whole thing over to the county.

"The paper said a monster killed him," the sister said in parting. "I'm not going to touch him." She hung up on Rosa.

Rosa called her parents in Santa Fe. She didn't want them finding out from somebody who read the L.A. papers that her name was splashed on the front page. Without going into details she explained what was going on.

"Come home," her mother pleaded. "You need to rest. The death of your student has been a shock to you. I can hear it in your voice."

"I can't, mamá. I've only got a week. I'm swamped with work."

She lied. It wasn't academic work she was thinking about, but revenge. She had promised to find the killers of her friends.

"You work too hard," her mother said.

"I'll see you this summer. Promise."

"Call us," her father said. "Y cuidate."

"I will. I love you both," Rosa said in parting.

She didn't feel right not telling them the whole story, but what had happened to José and Chuco was mysterious. She didn't want to worry them.

Finally she called Detective Dill.

"You were right about Chuco," Dill said. "Papers are saying there's a monster on the loose. You started this ChupaCabra mess. Just what in the hell are you up to?"

"I just want to find who killed my friends," Rosa replied. She asked what he knew about Malo, the crack pusher the kids had described.

"Malo?" Dill replied. "Doesn't ring a bell. As far as I know there's no Malo on my list. Does he go by another name?"

"El Hombre Malo the kids call him," Rosa said.

"Not much to go on," the detective mumbled. "I'll look into it."

Rosa hung up. Either he's lying, or he's not doing his job. Or did Indio have the wrong name?

Later, driving to Self-Help, she marveled at the people on the streets. She had always enjoyed driving through the barrios. They reminded her of home. Summer evenings when she walked on the plaza with her mom and dad, people stopped to say hello. Everyone knew the family, from the priest at the Guadalupe church to the local politicians who hung out at La Fonda.

The East L.A. barrio had the same feeling of familiarity. People knew each other. Neighbors visited their favorite shops and restaurants, women walked arm in arm to the mercado, old men stopped to chat, immigrants from Mexico hustled for jobs. A sense of community permeated the streets.

Those not from the neighborhood often forgot the barrio wasn't just a place for gangs, drive-by shootings, and drugs. A solid working-class community was its real heart. The newly arrived immigrants from Mexico and Central America added spice to the streets.

On the side streets the older residents kept their houses neat and tidy. Kids played in the street, or gathered in recreation centers or playgrounds. Soccer was fast overtaking baseball as the main sport. Like parents everywhere, families desired a safe place and a good education for their children. Neighbors knew each other, and they worked together.

The news media never covers this part of the barrio, Rosa thought. It's always just the bad news they splash on TV.

Mousey and Leo were waiting in front of Self-Help when Rosa drove up. "Where's Indio?" she asked.

"He didn't come," Mousey said as they jumped into the car.

"He thinks the ChupaCabra is a Skinwalker," Leo said. "He's not afraid of gang fights, but witches scare him."

"I know," Rosa said. She knew the fear of witches was real to Indio. He could face any danger as long as it didn't involve witchcraft.

The crack house they drove up to appeared doubly sinister in the dark. It stood at the end of a dead-end street; the surrounding houses seemed deserted.

A perfect place to sell the junk, Rosa thought. Even the streetlight was busted.

A dank breeze rustled in the weeds as they got out of the car. Rosa shivered. If you wanted to make a horror movie, this was the house to rent.

"What do you think?" Leo asked.

"Looks deserted," Mousey said. "And spooky."

"The crack dealers pulled out because of Chuco's death," Leo explained. "They'll be back."

"You two stay in the car," Rosa said, checking her flashlight.

"Okay," Mousey agreed and got back in the car.

"No, we have to go with the profe," Leo insisted.

"I'll stay and if somebody drives up, I'll honk three times," Mousey suggested. "Like in the movies."

"I'm going with you," Leo said, and took Rosa's hand.

"I can't let you—"

"I ain't letting you go alone," Leo insisted.

"Okay, let's go."

Leo glanced at Mousey. "Remember, honk."

The two women disappeared into the dark.

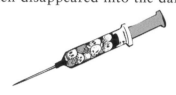

CHAPTER THIRTEEN

osa and Leo approached the front door cautiously. The house was dark and brooding, ostensibly empty, but Rosa sensed someone moving inside. Who?

The dry weeds rustled and Leo jumped.

"What was that?"

"Nothing," Rosa replied.

"I hope there aren't any snakes," Leo whispered as she clung to Rosa.

"The only snakes are the meth and crack dealers," Rosa said. She tried the front door. It was locked.

"We can't get in," Leo whispered. "Okay, let's go!"

"There must be a way," Rosa insisted. She tried a window; it didn't budge.

"Maybe the back door?" Leo suggested.

"Let's try it."

"One of us has to stay here," Leo said and gestured toward the car. "If Mousey sees us both disappear he might panic and start honking. I'll go. If I get in I'll open the door from the inside."

Rosa grabbed her arm and said, "I don't want you to go alone."

"There's no other way," Leo replied. "You want to get in or not? I'm not afraid."

Rosa reluctantly gave in. "Okay. Take the light. And be careful."

Leo took the flashlight and disappeared around the side of the house.

Seconds later Rosa heard the doorknob turning. "Leo?" she called as she pushed the door open.

"Leo?" she repeated, this time louder.

There was no answer.

Ah, playing games, Rosa thought. Okay, ready or not, here I come.

Rosa stepped inside. Her eyes adjusted to the dark as she walked into the large living room.

What did she expect to find? She didn't know, except she had a hunch about the painting she had seen.

Suddenly she realized Leo wasn't playing games, and she hadn't opened the door! She didn't have time to find the back door, open it, then come to the front to let Rosa in. Had someone else opened the door?

"Leo!" she called.

Her foot kicked something on the floor. An old Coke bottle. She picked it up and wished she had the flashlight as she turned to approach the painting.

In the faint light cast through the broken windows she could make out the sinister face of the man in the portrait. Something had moved.

Why was it lying against the wall instead of hanging?

Rosa looked at the eyes, the eyes that even in the dark seemed to stare back at her. Suddenly she knew!

She reached out, gripped the painting and pulled hard. The painting was a door that swung open! Instantly a large figure jumped out at her. The force of the assailant sent Rosa sprawling to the floor.

The attacker hissed. It stood over Rosa like a giant vampire ready to smother its victim. The eyes burned luminous in the dark.

"Malorio!" Rosa cried and hurled the Coke bottle. There was a dull thud followed by a cry of pain, and the figure turned and disappeared into the opening.

Rosa jumped to her feet. She heard the echoes of hurried footsteps as the attacker disappeared into the basement. Then all was quiet.

An escape route, Rosa thought. The large painting hid the entry to the basement. Police raids had not caught the pushers because they had a perfect escape route. The strong smells coming from the basement told Rosa that's where they cooked meth.

Was it Malorio who attacked her? She couldn't be sure, but those burning evil eyes brought back the image of the man.

"Leo!" Where was Leo?

Rosa hurried down the hallway toward the back of the house. Stumbling and crashing into things, she found the door and pushed it open. There at the doorstep lay Leo.

"Leo!" Rosa cried, gathering her into her arms.

She touched Leo's head and felt something warm. Blood. Leo was bleeding.

"Leo!" Rosa cried again, shaking the limp body.

Leo stirred, opened her eyes. "Oh, damn, what hit me?"

"Thank God," Rosa whispered. For a moment she thought the ChupaCabra had claimed another victim.

"What do you mean 'thank God'?" Leo scowled. "Somebody hit me."

"Who?"

"I didn't see him. Came from behind—" She felt her head. "Good thing I have a thick head."

"Can you get up?"

"I think so," she replied, and Rosa helped her to her feet. Did the monster behind the painting have somebody watching the back door? Rosa glanced at the chop shop. The hulks of cars rose like dead creatures in the dark. Whoever attacked Leo had plenty of time to escape.

"Lean on me—" Rosa said, picking up the light from the ground.

She was interrupted by the sound of her car horn.

"Mousey?"

"Maybe he's in trouble?"

They hurried around the side of the house in time to see the flashing red lights of a police car as it careened to a stop.

Officers jumped out, grabbed a terrified Mousey, and slammed him against the side of the car.

"I ain't done nothin'! I'm innocent!" Mousey cried.

"Shut up and keep your hands on the car, feet apart!" One of the officers shouted as he searched Mousey. "You're under arrest!"

Rosa recognized detective Dill's voice.

"He's with us," Rosa replied as she and the limping Leo approached the policemen.

Lights flashed in their direction, blinding them.

"Dr. Medina," Dill greeted her. "Just what in the hell are you doing here?"

"We were—" Rosa stammered. "We're doing research—"

"At night? Oh, I see. Looking for the ChupaCabra." Dill turned to his partner and laughed, a low, sarcastic laugh. "Dr. Medina believes we have a monster on the loose."

"Is this kid with you?" the officer asked.

"Yes. Let him go."

Dill nodded at the officer and he released Mousey. "And her?" He pointed at Leo.

"She's been hurt. She needs a doctor."

Dill shone his light on Leo's pale face, saw the streak of blood, and signaled to the officer.

"Need some first aid."

The cop helped Leo to the car, sat her down, and checked her wound.

"What happened?" Dill inquired.

"Somebody hit her," Rosa said. "Inside—"

"You were in the house?"

Rosa nodded.

"That's breaking and entering," Dill growled. "There's time in jail for that, you know."

"I didn't break and enter," Rosa replied. "Somebody opened the door and invited me in."

"There's someone in the house?" Dill asked. "Who?"

"I don't know. Whoever it was escaped into the basement and out the back."

"I've been in that house a dozen times," Dill said. "Never found a basement."

Probably didn't want to, thought Rosa.

"What else did you find?"

Rosa hesitated. Should she tell him about the attack? No, it was best to be cautious.

"Nothing. But tell me, Detective Dill, what brought you here tonight?"

The flashing lights of the police cars illuminated Dill's puffy red face. "I got a tip your ChupaCabra was in the neighborhood. If he comes into my turf I'm going to bust him." He laughed anew, and turning to his partner he said, "Come on. Let's check out her story."

"Your friend needs stitches," the cop said as he followed Dill.

"And quit playing detective!" Dill growled in parting. "Next time, I bust you all."

"Rosa," a pale Leo whined. "I want to go home."

"Hospital first," Rosa said, putting her arm around Leo and helping her into the car.

"Damn," Mousey said, "we almost got busted. You okay, Leo?"

"I'm okay."

"Who hit you?"

"ChupaCabra," Leo replied.

CHAPTER FOURTEEN

osa awakened from a haunting nightmare. The ChupaCabra had flown out of a dark tunnel and unfolded its large black wings; its fangs dripped blood. The fiery eyes were red like burning embers.

Beside her Leo stirred. After taking Leo to the hospital they had dropped Mousey off. Rosa insisted Leo spend the night with her in case she needed further medical attention.

"Buenos dias," Rosa said. "How did you sleep?"

"Bien. Y tu?"

Rosa said nothing about her nightmare. "Good. How's your head?"

Leo felt the top of her bandaged head. "A little headache, but I don't feel any pain. I heard someone behind me, so when I turned the blow glanced off my head. Otherwise—"

She didn't need to finish. Rosa knew a direct blow with a blunt instrument might have killed Leo. Why were people around her so susceptible to danger? Was Malorio's curse real?

"I'll get you some aspirin and orange juice. Then some strong coffee."

Later, while they munched on pan dulce and coffee, Leo talked about her life. Her parents had come from Mexico, seeking work. They worked as campesinos in the fields until her father saved enough to start a bakery on Avenida César Chávez near Ford Boulevard.

The family worked hard and prospered, but Leo had gotten into drugs in high school. She spent two years living on the streets, completely separated from her family.

"How did you start?" Rosa asked.

"The guy I used to go with. He pushed drugs at school, and I thought I was madly in love with him. So I started smoking with him, then we tried crystal."

"Crystal? Is that meth?" Rosa asked.

"Yeah. The shit has so many names, same fucking results. It's a rush. Don't let anyone fool you, it's a rush. That's why it's so easy to get hooked. Then I got pregnant."

Leo had never told Rosa this part of her past.

"Yeah, I didn't take care of myself. Once I tasted meth, that's all I lived for. I don't even know who the father was. We all did things together. You know, the sex was wild. But I sobered up a little, knew I couldn't raise a child...so I had an abortion."

She paused and stared at her coffee cup. Rosa reached across and held her hands. Tears came to Leo's eyes.

"Hardest thing I ever did. But I didn't have any options. I hadn't seen my family in years, so I didn't want to tell them I was pregnant. I made the decision on my own. That's also when I decided to get clean. I went to Self-Help and got counseling. And I went back to my familia. Funny thing, it wasn't that hard. They greeted me with open arms. My dad and mom cried when I walked into the bakery. So, with their help, and yours"— Leo squeezed Rosa's hands—"I'm staying clean."

"You'll make it," Rosa reassured her.

Her cell rang, Rosa glanced at the screen, and answered it.

A troubled Mousey said, "I'm over at Indio's place. You better come quick."

"Is he all right?"

"He's gone."

"What do you mean, gone?"

"Left a note. Something about the Skinwalker. Something about a curse. Can you come?"

"Be right over," Rosa replied, offing the phone. "Indio's gone," she said to Leo. "I need to get over there."

"I'll go with you."

"You sure you're feeling okay?"

"I'm okay. No pain, really."

"Vamos," Rosa said and they dashed out to her car.

Leo knew where Indio lived. He and two other young men rented a house not far from Self-Help on Rowan. Indio's friends were gone to work, but Mousey was waiting at the door for Rosa and Leo.

"Come in," Mousey said.

"Que pasó?" Rosa asked.

"I came by this morning, looking for Indio. Looks like he's gone home. He left this." He handed the note to Rosa.

Rosa read aloud. "Mousey, I didn't mean to run out on you, but I am afraid. Last night I checked the place where Chuco died. The man that walks on four legs is there. I swear I saw him. There's a curse here! The monster you call ChupaCabra is a Skinwalker. He saw me, so I'm next. I *need* to get home and see my uncle Billy. He is a medicine man. Be careful. All of you be careful."

Rosa looked at Leo and Mousey. "It's signed Charlie Joe Begay, Indio's name."

"One of the vatos next door was leaving for work when I got here. He saw Indio leaving. Didn't take anything with him, just got in his truck and left."

"What is this Skinwaker thing all about?" Leo asked.

Rosa told them what she knew. "The Navajo believe there are witches who dress in the skin of wolves. They use the hollow bone of a dead person to blow 'corpse dust' into their victims. That's how they make people sick."

"Corpse dust? You mean—"

Rosa nodded. "The bones of a dead person crushed into a powder."

"Damn," Leo said. "That's heavy. So these Skinwalkers can put a curse on anyone. Like a bruja. I read this book where witches put a hex on a man, and to get well he had to vomit a ball of hair. That's scary."

"Yes," Rosa answered. "The person who is cursed cannot eat, grows weaker and weaker, finally dies."

"And Indio saw one here? In East Los?" Mousey shook his head. "What the hell are those Navajo Skinwalkers doing in East Los?"

"People take their beliefs with them wherever they go," Rosa replied. "It's part of Indio's world, part of what he believes."

"Just like we believe in brujas who can do bad things," Leo said.

"I don't believe that stuff," Mousey scoffed.

"You don't have to believe it," Leo said and punched his shoulder. "If Indio believes in Skinwalkers then that's the way it is!"

"Do you *really* think that was ChupaCabra last night?" Mousey asked.

"No," Rosa said. "What I saw was a man. An evil man who can fly."

"Fly?" a puzzled Mousey asked.

"In airplanes. From Puerto Rico to Miami to Mexico to East L.A. They fly dope."

"International traficantes," Leo added.

"I get it," Mousey said. "It's what the politicians want. NAFTA. Globalized business. Globalized drugs!"

Yes, Rosa nodded. Mousey had put it together. International trade in illicit drugs. Destroy the brains of the young. La gente saw drugs destroy their families, and they gave it a name. The monster ChupaCabra reared its head in the barrios.

For centuries Mexican parents used la Llorona and the Cucúi to frighten their children, thus hoping to keep them out of harm's way. Now the families were fragmented, torn apart by poverty, torn apart by social forces far beyond their control. And there was a new monster, the ChupaCabra, and the stories of its horror were spreading.

"So what do we do?" Leo asked.

"We have to help Indio," Rosa replied. "If he believes he's being chased, then he needs help."

"He said he was going to his uncle, the medicine man," Mousey said, pointing at the note Rosa held in her hand.

"But if he doesn't get there in time..." Rosa shivered. Was Indio marked as the next ChupaCabra victim? Had the curse been passed to Indio? Had he really seen a Skinwalker at the crack house? Or ChupaCabra?

"Indio's heading home," Rosa said. "He's driving and he has a head start. I'm flying to New Mexico as soon as I can get a flight."

She hurried to her car, Mousey and Leo at her heels.

CHAPTER FIFTEEN

By late afternoon Rosa was on a Southwest flight out of L.A. Eddie drove her to the airport, but it was impossible for him to cancel the play and go with her.

"You shouldn't be going alone," he protested.

"I'll be okay," Rosa assured him. "I need to intercept Indio. I have to make sure he gets to his uncle."

"Can he help?"

"Yes. If Indio believes Skinwalkers are after him, the medicine man is his only hope. Besides, I can't stand by and do nothing."

"Cuidado," Eddie said.

"I'll be careful. Thanks for everything. Good luck on the play."

"You know how it is the last few days—details, details. Call me as soon as you know your return flight."

"Gracias, amigo." She hugged him, turned, and disappeared into the terminal.

She had calculated Indio's route. He would probably drive up to Barstow, then east on I-40 to Gallup. From there he would take state highway 666 north to the Tohatchi area. *The Devil's*

Highway, the natives called the road. Recently the state highway department had changed the number.

Rosa had calculated her itinerary to the hour. She would fly to Alburquerque, rent a car, and head for Gallup. She should get there just after sunset, and if her luck held, Indio would arrive there at the same time.

Mousey's description of Indio's '84 Toyota pickup truck, battered and held together with baling wire, could apply to a lot of trucks on the reservation. But Mousey said it sported an orange front fender. Most homes on the reservation didn't have street addresses, so Rosa would be looking for Indio's truck. After that, it would be a matter of pure luck if she found him.

It wasn't until the plane had taken off that she realized how irrational her plan was. She had a rough idea where Indio was headed and the description of his truck. That was it.

But she had to try. Malorio's curse had already struck twice. Two innocent men were dead.

She had picked up some of her research notes on the way out of the house, hoping to do some reading on the plane. But she couldn't concentrate. The papers lay limp on the folding tray in front of her. She closed her eyes and leaned back in her seat.

Her mind tried to make connections, search for causes and effects that might explain what had happened. It all had to do with Lago Negro, Malorio, and ChupaCabra.

And I'm at the center, she thought.

Someone, or some thing, was trying to scare her. In a very bad way. They were willing to kill José and Chuco. Why? What had she seen at Lago Negro that made her someone to be feared? And feared by whom?

And how about El Jefe, the man Alfredo said was connected to the flow of illegal drugs through Puerto Vallarta north into the United States? The DEA had cracked down on drug shipments along the Tijuana/San Diego area. Had the cartels found a new route?

What did José, Chuco, and Indio have in common? They knew her. And Detective Dill said both José and Chuco had been, at one time or another, into drugs.

The plane landed on time, and Rosa, carrying only an overnight bag, was quickly at the car rental counter. She was sorry not to call her parents, but she didn't want to worry them. How could she explain that she was chasing a young Navajo man who was fleeing L.A. because he thought the ChupaCabra was a Skinwalker out to get him?

She took I-40 west and half an hour later she dipped into the Río Puerco basin, an expanse of dry desert carved by wind erosion. The river itself, which flowed only when the cloud-bursts of summer struck, was just a dry arroyo on this March afternoon. Listening to the music on the radio didn't help to dissipate her worry. Would she be able to find Indio given the scant details she had?

The weight of night fell over the landscape. A faint band of orange streaked the western horizon, then faded. The dark shrouded the desert, the mesas, and the rock formations. The only sign of life was the constant buzz of traffic on the interstate.

Rosa glanced at the speedometer. She was doing ninety. Something was driving her to a rendezvous she couldn't miss. Indio's life hung in the balance.

She didn't stop in Grants, but by the time she reached Gallup she knew she needed the bathroom and coffee. Gallup, the trading capital for the Navajo reservation, was gaily lighted. Rosa parked in front of a small cafe, and, fighting a cold, blustery wind, she hurried inside. The restaurant was empty except for two state policemen at the counter. They glanced at Rosa, nodded as she walked past them, then returned to their roast beef dinner.

Rosa headed for the bathroom to freshen up. She felt tired, but she knew she had to push on. Indio's life might depend on her.

At the counter a young Navajo waitress filled Rosa's coffee cup and handed her a menu. "Getting cold out there," she said.

Outside bundled figures hurried along the sidewalk.

"Yes," Rosa replied.

The waitress smiled. "You from around here?"

"No, Santa Fe. I'm teaching in Los Angeles, but my family is from Santa Fe."

The waitress, with little to do, waited for more of Rosa's story.

"I'm on my way to Sanostee," Rosa added. "To visit a friend."

One of the policemen turned and looked at Rosa. "None of my business, lady, but did I hear you say you're headed for Sanostee?"

"Yes," Rosa replied.

"Well, drive slowly. There's a wreck just north of Tohatchi."

"Anybody hurt?"

"Nope. A truck is smashed up, but no passengers. The officer there thinks whoever was in the truck probably got a ride and left the truck."

"Or the driver wandered off into the desert," his fellow officer added. "Disappeared into thin air."

"Wouldn't be the first time that happened," the waitress said ominously.

"What do you mean?" Rosa asked.

The waitress shrugged. "Things happen out there. I'm glad I don't have to drive that road at night. More coffee?" She filled Rosa's cup.

"Was there a description of the truck?" Rosa asked.

"An '84 Toyota," the officer replied. "The kind that's been on the road many miles."

"Navajo limos," the waitress said, smiling halfheartedly.

The state troopers laughed. One finished slopping up the last of the gravy from his plate and said, "Held together with wire, uninsured, and usually been in a dozen accidents."

The year of the truck made Rosa sit up straight. "My friend drives an old Toyota," she said. "Was there more of the description?"

"Just old and beat up, a bright orange fender—"

"Orange fender!" Rosa gasped. She reached into her purse, tossed a five dollar bill on the counter, and dashed out the door.

"A young lady in a hurry," the state cop said as they looked after Rosa.

"Not good," the waitress whispered.

CHAPTER SIXTEEN

Rosa sped north, fearing she would arrive too late. The officer had described Indio's truck. What would she find?

North of Tohatchi, just before the Sanostee turnoff, she came upon a Navajo policeman. His car was parked on the shoulder of the road, behind the wrecked Toyota. Rosa pulled up and hurried to the policeman's car.

As she approached the officer rolled down his window. "Need help, lady?" he asked.

"Was anyone hurt in the wreck?" She pointed to the Toyota.

"Nope. Whoever was driving the truck is gone. There are tracks..." He pointed to a dirt road that branched off the pavement. "Do they belong to the driver?" she asked, thinking Indio had walked away from the wreck.

"Don't know. There are two sets of tracks."

Two? As far as Rosa knew Indio was traveling alone. Maybe he had picked up a hitchhiker.

"Do you know who the truck belongs to?" the officer asked.

"Charlie Joe Begay."

The officer held up the registration. "Yup. Friend of yours?"

"A student. We need to help him."

"Is he in trouble?"

What could Rosa say? Indio is fleeing from a Skinwalker. We need to find him before the witches do.

"No, not trouble," she stammered.

"I can't help him if I can't find him."

"We need to search for him."

The officer shook his head. "Don't have time. I've got to get to Tohatchi. Besides, I don't think there's foul play here. No blood, no signs of alcohol involved. Charlie is probably okay. Maybe he caught a ride home—"

"But you said there were tracks on that road."

"If he headed out there it means he knows there's a sheep camp nearby. It won't freeze tonight. He'll be all right."

"I have to find him," Rosa pleaded.

"Why?"

"He needs help," was all she could muster.

"Medical help?"

No, she thought, shaking her head. Spiritual help.

"I can come back in the morning," the officer volunteered. "Right now I've got to respond to a call from Tohatchi." He hesitated. "You're not thinking of going out there?" He nodded vaguely in the direction of the tracks.

"Yes."

"You got a flashlight?"

"No. I rented a car in Alburquerque."

He shook his head. "Look, lady, you can't go out there unprepared. A person can get lost—"

"I'm going," Rosa insisted.

"Damn," he whispered, fished into the glove compartment, and handed her a flashlight. "Far as I can tell the tracks go up that dirt road. About half a mile there's a box canyon, an outcropping of rocks. Old Billy Begay has a sheep camp there. Maybe that's where Charlie Joe headed."

"Billy Begay," Rosa repeated.

"Yeah. Charlie probably knows Billy."

Rosa thanked the officer. That was it! Indio had gone to his uncle!

"I wouldn't go there if I were you," the officer said in parting.

Rosa didn't ask why. She understood that she had been warned, and that he could tell her no more. Something mysterious was going on in the vicinity—something the police could not fix.

He shook his head, rolled up his window, and pulled away.

Rosa got in her car and drove down the rutted road. The path came to an abrupt end in a wide arroyo. Rosa got out and zipped up her leather jacket. Ahead of her rose the formation of rocks the officer had described.

Flashlight in hand, she crossed the sandy arroyo and headed toward rocks that resembled a natural amphitheater. Eons of windblasting had produced some of the most spectacular scenery in the desert, and here it had carved out a sandstone theater.

Rosa heard voices, then spotted the flicker of a fire reflecting on the rocks. She turned off her flashlight and approached cautiously. When she peered over the edge of a large boulder she saw Indio and an old man sitting in front of a campfire.

The old man was chanting. Across from him sat Indio, his eyes closed. The old man's song was a ceremony to help Indio. Had Indio seen the Skinwalker? The old man rocked back and forth as he sang.

What Rosa saw next sent a chill through her body. A pebble's toss away stood a man in the skin of a wolf. A Skinwalker watching Indio and his uncle!

"Blessed Mary!" Rosa cried and flipped on the flashlight, illuminating the man. He turned and rushed at her, pushing her into the sand. The creature's eyes flashed murder; claws slashed at Rosa. She ducked and in the same motion struck back with the flashlight.

The wolf mask slipped momentarily. In the dim light cast by the fire Rosa thought she recognized the face.

"Dill!" she cried.

The wolf man growled and struck again; the blow sent Rosa to the ground. For a moment he stood over her, raising a gnarled claw to strike. Then someone called, and the wolf man turned and disappeared into the night.

Within seconds a very surprised Indio was at her side. "Teach? What are you doing here?" He helped her up.

"Looking for you," Rosa replied.

"What the hell was that?" he asked. He looked into the dark where the man had disappeared.

"Who is it, Charlie Joe?" Indio's uncle called as he came hurrying up.

"My teacher," Indio replied.

The old man looked at Rosa. "Are you hurt?"

"No, I'm okay," Rosa said, dusting herself off and picking up her flashlight.

"What knocked you down?"

"A wolf man," Rosa replied.

The old man shrank back from touching her. "This is bad," he mumbled. "To be touched by a Skinwalker is very bad. You will need a ceremony. Only in this way can we give you a stone that protects you."

"I have protection," Rosa replied, touching the cross at her throat.

"Oh, a Christian," the old man smiled. "A good faith, but not as strong as the old prayers. Come." He motioned. "The man who walks on four legs is gone. He will not be back tonight. Come."

He turned and led them to his hut.

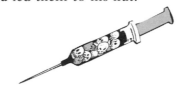

CHAPTER SEVENTEEN

The old man's hut was made of piñon and juniper branch es. It sat against the sandstone cliff, which provided excellent protection from northerly winter blasts. Around the side were the sheep pens.

The old man lit a kerosene lantern and stirred the fire in the small stove.

"I can't believe it's you," Indio said. He looked at Rosa with admiration. "How did you know I would be here? How did you find me?"

"We got your note and I followed you," Rosa answered, shivering.

"You're cold," Indio's uncle said. He put an old Navajo blanket around her shoulders. "Coffee will warm you up."

Rosa thanked him.

"You could be in trouble," Indio said.

"No more than you," Rosa replied.

"I mean with the Skinwalker." Indio glanced at his uncle and the old man shook his head.

"Yenaaloshi," he whispered. "Not good. But don't worry, I can take care of those witches."

Rosa didn't tell them she thought the so-called Skinwalker might be an LAPD detective. The idea that she had seen Dill dressed in the skin of a wolf was absolutely improbable. Had the face simply resembled Dill? Maybe there *was* witchcraft going on and only Indio's uncle understood it. Some practition-ers of ancient magic could take the shape of animals. Rosa had heard such witch stories from her parents. People from the old Hispano villages told how witches took the form of owls to fly at night. But could such things happen today?

"Why did you come?" Indio asked.

"I told you, I was worried about you."

"That your ChupaCabra might get me?"

"Yes."

Indio's uncle poured three cups of steaming coffee. The brew had been on the stove all day; it was thick, strong, and invigorating.

"This is my uncle Billy," Indio said. Then in Navajo he told the uncle about Rosa, his teacher from Los Angeles.

"I am glad to meet such a brave woman," Uncle Billy said. "Welcome to my home. You are safe here."

"Thank you. Good coffee."

"Navajo special." Uncle Billy beamed.

"What caused the wreck?" Rosa asked.

Indio looked at his uncle. The uncle nodded. It was okay for his nephew to tell the brave woman his story.

"To understand what happened tonight you have to know a little about me. I grew up here. In the summers I used to help Uncle Billy herd sheep. I didn't care much for school. I liked to roam around. There was a very rich man who tried to get my uncle to move his sheep away. He wanted to use this land to pasture his own herd. My uncle said no. One night I saw the man blowing some witch objects at my uncle."

"The man was yenaaloshi," Uncle Billy explained. "He took the hollow bone of a dead person and blew the evil powders into me. For a long time I was sick. Many chants were sung for me, and I was finally cured."

Rosa had heard that witches used hollow bones, probably an arm bone taken from a dead person, to blow a witching object into their victims. Only a witch would dare touch the bones of a dead person. The powders they blew into the victim made him sick. The object-that-caused-sickness could only be taken out by a medicine man.

Blowing evil through the hollow bone reminded Rosa that Chuco had described how addicts roll up a dollar bill to snort cocaine. The ill-gotten gain, the dollar bill, was like the hollow bone. The cocaine was a "witch" powder ruining many lives.

"That rich man was a Skinwalker," Indio continued. "He saw me, and so I knew he would come after me. I ran away to Gallup. I thought I could escape from him. I started drinking a lot, got into trouble. One night a *man-walking-like-a-wolf* was following me along the railroad tracks. I had to run farther away, so I headed for L.A. But that was no good. I kept on drinking and doing drugs."

"So when you saw the wolf at the crack house you thought he had returned to get you?" Rosa said.

Indio nodded. "I knew I had to get back here."

"He needs a five-day chant," Uncle Billy said. "Tonight I had a feeling. I went to the road. There I saw the man-who-walks-on-four-legs lay a trap. I saw Charlie Joe fall into their trap. The car flew up, then fell. The evil ones thought they had him, but I was there first. I pulled Charlie Joe from the truck and brought him here. With very few preparations I began to sing."

So the two sets of footprints the Navajo officer had described belonged to Indio and his uncle. "What did the truck hit?" Rosa asked.

"Witch trap," was all the uncle would say. "Tomorrow I go for help. Some friends to do the sandpainting, maybe a good singer to come and help me." He gazed at Rosa across the table, his grey eyes shining with mystery. "Tomorrow we will chant over you."

"I thank you, but I have to return home," Rosa said. "Friends need my help." She knew she couldn't stay, as much as she'd like to participate in the sing.

The two men glanced at each other. Perhaps the woman didn't understand how strong the curse was. She needed the curing power of a ceremony. But then, she wasn't Navajo, so maybe she would take care of it in her own way.

"What about the man who attacked me?" she asked.

"That was not a man," Uncle Billy said.

"I thought I saw a man." Rosa pushed her case. The wolf mask had slipped, she had seen a face. Or was it only her imagination? She told the uncle about the ChupaCabra mystery.

"You speak of ChupaCabra," Uncle Billy said. "It is an evil that has come to your people. You wish to solve the mystery, so you ask yourself: *who is ChupaCabra*? I say these are bad witches who take the shape of ChupaCabra. They come to your children and turn them away from the True Path. Long ago these people of power could change into animal bodies. They could do good or bad. Now they only do bad. Now the world believes in violence. Even the governments and some of the religious leaders believe only in violence. Long ago the witches turned into animal forms. Now they turn into ChupaCabra. Used by evil men to harm your children. You must protect yourself."

"How do I protect myself?" Rosa asked.

"As we protect Charlie Joe," the uncle replied. "We will prepare a sandpainting, and we will sing. These are the old healing ceremonies that came to us from our ancestors. If you cannot stay, give me something you treasure and I will place it on the sandpainting. The healing will work its way to you. Much like your Christian prayers."

Rosa hesitated then took the cross from around her neck and handed it to the uncle.

"Good. Now the night is growing old. The clouds have wrinkled the face of the moon. The wind calls and the coyotes answer. It is time to rest."

He took well-worn sheepskin and blankets and spread them in a corner.

"You can sleep here. Safe. If your ChupaCabra comes, I will shoot it with my rifle."

He grinned and Rosa had to smile. "Thank you," she said, and without argument she crawled into the warm blankets.

The odor of sheep was strong in the hut, but the aroma of cedar wood burning in the stove reminded her of winter evenings at home when her father lit the fireplace. After dinner the family would stroll to the Santa Fe plaza, and the fragrance of piñon smoke was soul-satisfying. How serene and how far away those childhood nights seemed!

Outside the sheep bleated softly from time to time. In the distance, the yipping of coyotes carried in the wind.

She heard Indio and his uncle whispering into the night, and she felt safe. She fell into a sound sleep, the best she had had in a long time. That night the recurring dream did not disturb her. She awoke refreshed.

Indio stood over the stove, cooking eggs and strips of mutton and warming tortillas.

"Good morning," he said when Rosa stirred. "Uncle has gone to tell friends we are having a sing. The bathroom is outside, and there's a bowl of water for washing."

"Thank you," Rosa replied. "I slept so soundly—"

"Country air," Indio said.

Rosa stepped out into a brilliant morning. It was cold, but the sun shone across the desert. A trace of spring rain hung in the air.

The bathroom was an outhouse, and the bowl of water in which she washed her face was cold. Uncle Billy had even put out a fresh bar of soap and a clean towel for her.

The cold water and the rough towel felt wonderful on her face. She was grateful for this moment of simplicity. Perhaps only here could men like Uncle Billy carry on their traditions and pray against the evil he said encircled the world.

While they ate Rosa asked Indio about his plans.

"Not L.A.," he replied. "I'm home. After the sing I'll help my uncle with the sheep. Lambing season is here. Maybe I can learn his curing ceremonies."

"Many of us dream of returning to the homeland," Rosa said. "Few of us can."

"You helped. You came here because you knew I was in trouble. I appreciate that."

"You're not afraid now," Rosa said.

"No, not afraid anymore. When I hit the trap on the road, I thought I was going to die. But my uncle was there. He pulled me out of the truck. He's got stronger medicine than men-who-walk-on-four-legs."

"Yes, he does," Rosa agreed. "You can learn a lot from him."

"Maybe you should stay. My uncle's ceremony can get rid of the ChupaCabra curse."

"Maybe," Rosa replied. "My way is different from yours, but I'm sure his songs will help you."

After breakfast Rosa said goodbye and walked back to where she had left her car. When she passed the place where she had been attacked, she paused. Her foot prints were clear on the clean, desert sand. She walked around, carefully studying the ground. What she saw made the back of her neck prickle.

There on the sand were the clear tracks of a wolf, or as Uncle Billy would say, a man-who-walks-on-four-legs. Yenaaloshi.

CHAPTER EIGHTEEN

By nine Rosa was on the road to Gallup. Once she was on I-40, she called her parents. She wanted to see them, and she needed the sense of love and security they had always provided.

At Alburquerque she turned north, and an hour later, much to the surprise and delight of her father and mother, she was having lunch with them in Santa Fe. She told them as much as she dared about the events of the past few days. When she was done her mother spoke.

"Evil has always been in the world," she said. "But now it's worse. So much violence. The Bible tells us it would come to this."

Her father was more of a pragmatist.

"Sometimes what happens is unexplainable. Remember those mutilated cattle at my primo's ranch. That kind of thing has happened around the state, and nobody can explain it. Some of the old timers say it's aliens from spaceships. The Navajos call it witchcraft. Maybe the ChupaCabra came to New Mexico."

"You're teasing," Rosa said, reaching for her father's hand.

"The way I figure it, we project our inner fears."

"And they become stories," Rosa said.

"Sometimes the projections become real," he mused. "Don't we all have our demons? It's part of being human. Like the poet said, you can't just have angels on your shoulder, there's also a diablito. They argue about who will get you. Kids on drugs have lost the argument."

"What can we do?" Rosa asked.

"All we can do is what you're doing: help the kids. Let them know there's a good path in life."

"We are proud of you," her mother said. "But we worry. Los Angeles is so far away. And we hear about the gang fights."

"Violence begets violence," Rosa's father added.

"Oh, let's not talk about negative things," her mother interjected. "You're here and that's all that matters. But you need to get out. Enjoy the day. Why don't you go see Father Larry? We told him you would be here for spring break, and he said you wouldn't dare leave without seeing him."

"How is he?"

"He's happy as can be. We're so glad he's here. And you know, he always admired you."

"I want to see him," Rosa said. "A walk will do me good."

Her plane to L.A. didn't leave until late that evening, so she had plenty of time to enjoy the respite. A walk around the plaza would feel good. And, after all, the place was home.

Outside, a warm spring breeze had descended over Santa Fe, gathering the city in its embrace. Santa Feans headed for the plaza to enjoy the March sun. Old timers sat on the benches and discussed politics and the weather. Rosa turned toward the Santuario de Nuestra Señora de Guadalupe to say hello to Father Larry.

When he opened the door, he shouted her name and lifted her in a bear hug.

"Rosa Medina! I didn't know you were in town. It's great to see you. Just last Sunday I talked to your parents. They said you might be coming home. Come in, come in. I was having coffee.

My own blend. Santa Fe has gotten so worldly now we can order our own blend of coffee at the deli. I love it. So how are you?"

"I'm well," Rosa said, "and you?"

"I feel great. I love being a priest. Imagine, I got to come back home. Of course serving the Lord means I had to give you up—"

He winked. Rosa and Larry Ortiz had grown up in the same neighborhood. Even though Larry was older, their parents had hoped that they might eventually marry. But it wasn't to be. Larry went off to the seminary and later Rosa entered college.

"And you? How's teaching?"

"I love it," Rosa said, and after catching him up on the recent twists and turns of her career, she told him about José and Chuco. Father Larry offered his condolences.

"ChupaCabra," he said thoughtfully. "I read something about a Puerto Rico incident. Then Mexico. But the beast was only killing chickens and goats. Now it's killing humans."

Rosa nodded.

"The devil uses many disguises," Father Larry said. "As far as I know the ChupaCabra doesn't appear in the folklore of New Mexico. But there are other scary creatures. Every New Mexico village has its own boogeyman. Or bruja. I've heard stories of witches who fly in old-fashioned washtubs, creatures who are ten feet tall, ogres who wait under bridges, and of course there's always la Llorona and the Cucúi. I always thought these were fantasy creatures invented by parents to keep us kids in line."

"They're partly that," Rosa agreed. "We frighten our children into behaving. The Coco or la Llorona will get you if you are a malcriado."

"It used to work." Father Larry nodded. "Now the kids can't be frightened into anything. Too many horror movies, too much TV. Maybe those creatures represent ancestral spirits who are displeased. So they come to frighten us."

"Ancestral spirits are kind," Rosa mused. "Drugs are the work of evil people."

"I heard witchcraft stories all my life, but I never paid much attention. I always thought a blessing would take care of such things." He paused. "But what you saw last night, perhaps it was caused by fatigue. You had been traveling all day, your young friend was in danger, the stress—"

Rosa nodded. Yes, all that was possible. But she had seen something. What?

Father Larry cleared his throat. "I'm sorry I'm not much help. I haven't had much experience with curses or witches. Till this winter." He stood and paced. "A young woman took ill at a ranch near Trampas. The word got around that it was witchcraft. The family called me. I left in a hurry, so I forgot to pack a crucifix. Of course the family had a rosary and a crucifix in their home, but the father of the girl, a strange man, told me to use this."

He reached into his desk and took out a knife. He pressed the button and the blade swished to life, the steel glistening in the light.

"It's an old pachuco switchblade, but look closely. Engraved on the handle is a beautiful cross. The father insisted I use the knife. *To cut away the evil that possessed his daughter*, he said. I blessed the knife, then I placed it at the head of the bed where the girl lay. I prayed all night. Sometime in the early morning hours I saw something, like a shadow, rise from the girl. I felt helpless as I watched the ghost-like figure writhe in agony, then disappear. I was astounded. The girl got well. The next day she was up and around. The father thanked me and gave me the knife. 'Someday you will give it to someone who needs to cut away the evil' he said. Anyway, I want you to have it. To protect you."

He handed the knife to Rosa. "I'm sorry, it's all I have to offer."

"Thank you," Rosa said, taking the knife. She looked at it and felt its balance. As a tomboy she had carried a knife, just like the neighborhood boys she grew up with. They played along the Santa Fe River, and Rosa was usually the leader. But that was long ago.

Rosa remembered a story. "My dad told me that a woman from Chimayó once used a knife to slice the air in front of a gigantic hail storm. She turned the storm away and saved the crops."

"Miracles happen," Father Larry said.

She thanked Father Larry and put the knife in her bag. "I'll come by the next time I'm home. Take you to dinner at Tomasita's."

"That's a deal," Father Larry said, smiling. "It's so good to see you."

After they parted, Rosa ambled toward the plaza. For the moment, she was swept up in the good feelings of the day. She stopped to buy gifts from the vendors who lined the portal of the governor's original home. A bolo tie for Eddie, a ring for Mousey, earrings for Leo, a small painting for her parents.

But she had trouble getting into the spirit of the spring day; she sensed something wasn't right. As she neared La Fonda she realized what it was. She was being followed, and the person following her was not a friend. Rosa felt goosebumps.

That's it, she told herself. All morning I've had the feeling I'm not alone. She paused in front of a store window and used the glass as a mirror. The shadow behind her quickly disappeared into a doorway.

She crossed the street and entered La Fonda. The lobby of the hotel was noisy and full of tourists. She ducked into the newspaper stand. From there she had a view of lobby where a group of healthy-looking Anglos were exchanging skiing stories. Another rowdy bunch sat at the bar, drugstore cowboys chasing Dallas matrons, and politicians plotting how to get the governor. A Pueblo woman walked by, selling kachina dolls. At a small table sat a young woman reading Tarot cards for a young man who seemed more interested in her than the revelation the cards held.

The man who had been following Rosa hurried by. He wore a jacket and a scarf and a wide-brimmed hat pulled low, so she couldn't see his face.

As he passed by her Rosa shouted, "Hey!"

Without turning he made a dash for the exit.

Rosa followed the man down the hall to the parking garage. When she opened the door two tall, scroungy looking cowboys stood in her path.

"Hi, lady," one of the them roared, blocking Rosa's way. "What's your hurry?"

Rosa tried to duck around him, but the second huge man wouldn't budge. "Why not join us for a little cheer!" He laughed.

They had her trapped, allowing the man she was following to disappear into the garage.

"Pendejos!" Rosa shouted, and pushed past them.

The men roared with laughter. "What a purty filly," one said. "I'd like to throw my saddle on her!"

"You're too ugly, Brad! You probably scared her to death."

Rosa hurried down the row of parked cars, searching for the man. Suddenly a truck came roaring toward her, tires squealing.

Rosa jumped aside and pasted herself against a parked car. The truck missed her by inches. As it went by she caught sight of the man behind the wheel.

"Dill!" she exclaimed. She was sure the man who had almost run her over was Frank Dill.

She was trembling with fear and anger. "The sonofabitch tried to kill me."

CHAPTER NINETEEN

Rosa slipped into a patisserie and ordered a glass of water.

Was it Dill I saw? Why would he try to run me over? Am I imagining things? Am I losing it?

Around her tourists and natives waiting for their pastries buzzed like honeybees at spring lilacs, but their antics didn't interest Rosa. She stared into space and wondered if she was hallucinating. Danger lay in her path, and maybe she was just attributing it to men who seemed to have something to do with the ChupaCabra.

"Are you ready to order?" the young waiter asked.

"What? No, thanks for the water," Rosa replied and hurried out.

Outside, the fresh air helped. She paused at the corner and looked for the truck. All was calm—of course it was gone by now.

Should she go to the police and file a complaint? What would she say: "A detective from the L.A. police department followed me to Santa Fe and tried to run me over in the La Fonda parking garage."

Preposterous!

Reaching home, she felt safe. Her mother had prepared an early dinner. She didn't tell them about the incident at La Fonda. They would only worry, and Rosa wasn't quite sure if the man in the car was Detective Dill or just a wild Santa Fe driver.

Parting with her parents was difficult. She convinced them, and herself, that she had a lot of school work to do. They protested. They wanted her to stay. Spring break was supposed to be a week of rest, but Rosa insisted she had too much to do. One day's visit was better than none.

"Are you sure you're going to be okay?" her father asked as they stood by her car. "This thing that's happening doesn't sound good to me."

"I will be, Dad," Rosa replied. "Really."

"Oh, I wish you could stay, mija," her mother pleaded. "I have a bad feeling—"

"This summer I'll come for a long visit."

"We can go camping in the Pecos Wilderness. God's country," her father said. And when he embraced her he whispered, "Cuídate."

"Que Dios te bendiga," her mother blessed her. Her eyes were wet as she parted from her daughter.

"Adios, see you this summer." Rosa waved and backed her car out of the driveway.

She drove to Alburquerque, turned in her rental car, and called Eddie before she caught her flight to L.A. He was waiting to pick her up at LAX.

"Rosa!" He hugged her. "Good to see you, mujer. How are you?"

"I'm good," Rosa replied. "And you? How are rehearsals coming?"

"Great. The cast is ready. Jorge Huerta came by. Can you imagine? El mero critic de Chicano theater! He gave us some good feedback. But what about you? Did you find Indio?"

"I found him. He's okay."

"Hey, you look tired. Long trip, huh?"

"Yeah, a long trip." A trip into another world, she thought.

On the drive home she told Eddie about her meeting with Indio and his Uncle Billy.

"Damn. That's scary," he said. "But why Indio?"

"He saw the Skinwalker at the crack house where Chuco died. There's a connection to what's happening."

"I don't get it," Eddie said.

"I don't either," she said and described the incident in the parking garage.

"Dill? What in the hell would Dill be doing in Santa Fe? And why try to run you down?"

"I don't know."

"Something's not making sense. You thought you saw Malorio at the crack house, then Dill at the curing ceremony and at the garage..." He glanced at Rosa.

"You think I've lost it? I've gone bananas?"

"Come on, I'm not saying that, Rosa, but those three men don't seem to have anything to do with each other. Mira, you've been under a lot of stress. José and Chuco's deaths, the trip to New Mexico, those dreams you've been having..."

Eddie was right. She was tired, and the grief she felt for José and Chuco hadn't been allowed to run its natural course. Her emotions were blocked inside. She had lost track of time and it seemed she had been on the road for weeks, months. She was running on empty. No wonder she felt exhausted.

"Since José died, you've been pushing yourself. You've got to rest. Take time out for yourself. The deaths were a shock, but you don't realize it yet. You're on this ChupaCabra thing, as if it mattered."

"It matters that I find out who killed José and Chuco."

"I don't know," Eddie's voice echoed with concern. "The whole thing seems to be getting out of hand. Maybe you should just leave it to the cops."

"Speaking of cops," Rosa answered, "can your friend at LAPD find out if Detective Dill was working today?"

"There you go again, see? You won't stop!"

"Please, Eddie, it's important. If he was here today then I imagined him in Santa Fe. It will help clear things."

"Yeah, sure. I'll call Bobby. That's easy enough. It's you I'm concerned about."

"Thanks, Eddie, I really do appreciate it. But I have to do something. I can't let José and Chuco down. What do you know about Bobby Mejía?" Rosa asked.

"You mean can he be trusted? Yeah. He grew up in the barrio, went to UCLA, got a degree in criminology or something like that. He worked his way up in LAPD. It's not easy being a Chicano in the system. They don't have a good rep in the barrio. But guys like Bobby are changing that. They stay in touch with la gente. They don't forget their roots. Every Saturday he's out helping in programs for the kids, working with Parks and Recreation."

"Sounds like a cool vato."

"He is. And he's handsome. He did a stint with the movies for awhile. But he really likes police work." Eddie pulled in front of Rosa's apartment. "Here we are, safe and sound."

"Come in."

"You're tired—"

"I'm also hungry. I'll fix sandwiches and coffee."

He took her bag. "Sounds good to me. I haven't had a bite since breakfast."

At her apartment door Rosa hesitated. Something didn't feel right. There was a smell in the air, dank and mysterious, with a whiff of sulfur in it. The smell brought back images of Lago Negro and Malorio's curse.

"What is it?" Eddie asked.

"Nada," Rosa replied, pushing open the door.

She flipped on the light and stared into a mess. Someone had ransacked her apartment.

"Oh my God," she cried.

Eddie went ahead of her. "Wait here," he said, walked in, then down the hall to the bedroom. "Whoever did this is gone," he said when he returned. "Hijo, they left a mess."

Rosa nodded. Drawers were open, the futon cushions scattered, things strewn all over the floor, even the kitchen cabinets had been emptied.

"Same thing in your bedroom and bath," Eddie said. "Probably locos looking for TV sets to sell for drug money!" He picked up a cushion and tossed it on the sofa.

"They didn't take the TV set." Rosa pointed. "Or my computer." She hurried to her bedroom. Her jewelry case was emptied on the floor, but none of her earrings or bracelets were missing. Whoever broke into her apartment hadn't come to steal TV sets or jewelry. They were after something else.

CHAPTER TWENTY

The following morning a very tired Rosa dragged herself to her friend's office. Cristina Molina and Rosa had attended UC Santa Barbara at the same time. After graduation Cristina had set up a counseling business in East L.A.

She helped develop a workshop for barrio kids for the Puente Project. Her "Knowledge of Self" program began by introducing young people to world myths. The focus was on the role of the hero in the ancient legends. Each student made a careful examination of the obstacles the hero faced in the course of his or her adventures; they paid close attention to the hero's virtues and personality traits.

Then they collected oral histories from their parents and grandparents. They quickly learned from these stories of hard work and survival that their parents had performed heroic deeds. The struggle to immigrate to a new country produced heroes. The hero acted for the good of the family and the community. The hero actually embodied the culture.

The kids looked closely at their own lives and saw the challenges they faced. They developed strategies to deal with problems. As one young man said during the early part of the workshop: "Hey, we poor Mexicans have heroes? Wow!"

Someone added: "Yeah, Jesus, César Chávez, Corky González, Martin Luther, and that guy Odee-sus."

"And la Virgen de Guadalupe, la Llorona, Selena, Frida Kahlo."

"And Pedro Infante. I read *Loving Pedro Infante*."

"How about Emily Dickinson? Does she count?"

"Sure, why not?"

"Mother Teresa. And St. Ann. My mom loves St. Ann."

A girl added: "Our parents are heroes."

They read Mesoamerican mythology. The stories from their own part of the world were, as they said, "totally awesome."

"Azteca warriors."

"Why not? Everyone with heart can be a warrior."

Yes, Rosa thought, Cristina was making a difference in the community. She hadn't seen her friend in months, but now was the time.

Cristina greeted Rosa at the door of her office on Whittier Boulevard. The office was only blocks from the Silver Dollar, the bar where Rubén Salazar had been killed by an L.A. County sheriff's deputy during the Chicano Moratorium. Ricardo López had tried to save the Silver Dollar because of its historic importance, but funding was scarce and he had to give up his dream.

The history of la gente reverberated on every street. Rosa could feel it. But it had to be saved if the young were to learn it. Maybe someday Ricardo would write a novel about the killing of Rubén Salazar.

"Rosa!" Cristina greeted her friend, embracing her warmly. "It's so good to see you, girl. It's been so long. You look great."

"No, I don't," Rosa replied, smiling.

"Okay, you look like a lowrider ran you over. So come in and tell me what's happening. I saw the paper and called you, but all I get is your answering machine. You've been gone?"

"It's a long story," Rosa replied.

"Yeah, and here I am with diarrhea of the mouth. It's just that I'm so glad to see you, mujer."

"And I'm glad to see you. But—"

"Say no more," Cristina comforted her friend, leading her into the consulting room. "Have a drink. Then we can talk. Sit here." She pointed to a comfortable chair. "What would you like to drink?"

"Have you got a bottle of tequila?"

Cristina smiled. "That bad, huh?"

"Tea will do."

"I've got some wonderful te de limón, freshly brewed. I stopped by the mercado this morning."

She served Rosa a cup of tea, saw to it that she was comfortable, then sat back to listen. Rosa told the entire story, beginning at Lago Negro and ending last night at her ransacked apartment.

When she was done Cristina sat in silence. "Niña, you have been to hell and back."

"That's how I feel," Rosa admitted. "I think Eddie made me realize just how tired I am. I haven't been able to face José's or Chuco's death. So maybe it's the stress—"

"Go on," Christina said softly.

"Maybe I'm just imagining things. Like the detective trying to run me over in Santa Fe. Like the Skinwalker at the ceremony for Indio."

"You're asking, are they real or hallucinations?"

Rosa sighed. "Yes."

Again Cristina waited, then whispered. "José is dead."

"Yes."

"Chuco is dead."

"Yes."

"You were in New Mexico, at Uncle Billy's place, and later in Santa Fe with your parents."

"Yes."

"Someone tried to run you down in the hotel garage?"

"Yes."

"That's a lot of reality, mujer," Cristina said.

"What about the Skinwalker who attacked me? And the vampire-like creature of the crack house? And Malorio at Lago Negro?"

"What about them?" Cristina asked.

"Did I see those—those monsters?"

"Are they monsters?"

Rosa thought, then answered softly. "They're men. I recognize them. But what about my nightmares?"

"When did they begin?"

Rosa hesitated. She hadn't thought of her nightmares being connected to any particular time or event.

"It was during my first visit to Lago Negro. A goat had been killed by the ChupaCabra; the Mexican newspapers created a big story over the incident. So I flew down to Puerto Vallarta. That's when I met Herminio and Lupe, and Alfredo. Alfredo took me into the jungle to see the goat. I took some photographs."

"Go on."

Rosa became more animated. The images were returning.

"I assumed, like the rest of the villagers, that the ChupaCabra sucked the goat's blood. There was even talk of a vampire monster. The villagers said he came every night. They could hear him flying overhead. That's it!"

"Go on . . . "

"The following evening I went back into the jungle alone. It got dark. I saw a truck parked at the clearing. I crept close . . . I saw a cage . . . something moved inside—I saw something hideous!"

"What?" Cristina asked, holding her friend's hands.

"The ChupaCabra! Eyes burning like fire! Then Malorio came up behind me and grabbed me. 'Now you have seen the ChupaCabra,' he shouted, 'you are cursed. *You cannot escape the curse of el ChupaCabra*!' That night I had the first nightmare. It's all coming back!" Rosa paused and looked plaintively at her friend. "Did he curse me? Is that what's haunting me?"

Cristina nodded. "Whatever you saw frightened you. You were literally 'scared to death.' Susto, my grandma used to call it. Fright creates a shock to the nervous system. You were in his territory, and he had control over you. He cursed you, and you weren't prepared to resist him. It was dark, you had seen the beast in the cage, he grabbed you, and in that moment of intense fear your subconscious accepted Malorio's curse. Now it appears in the form of your nightmares."

Cristina paused. Neither spoke. She got up and refilled the tea glasses.

"It makes sense," Rosa said. "But am I so weak? Can somebody really brainwash me?"

"It's not weakness," Cristina replied. "You were vulnerable and violated. In that state the curse became real. Like our kids who get into drugs. They, too, are vulnerable. For some the power of peer pressure leads them to experiment with drugs. At any moment of deep stress—and so many of our kids are under stress—suggestion can control the mind. It happens to presidents, famous artists, and the ordinary guy on the street that has one too many beers on the way home."

Rosa nodded.

"No, you're not weak, you're strong. You've been through a lot. Now that you know the source of the nightmares, you can process it out."

"Put ChupaCabra out of my mind?" Rosa asked.

"That may not be easy," Cristina replied. "You have an obsession to find the answer to the mystery. And it's very real because you want to find the murderers of José and Chuco. You also have to deal with the curse."

"How?" Rosa asked.

"Talking helps," Cristina replied. "I'm here to listen. We can work through everything that's happened. You have incredible strength inside, amiga. You can beat the curse."

"Just being here has already helped," Rosa acknowledged. "Gracias."

Rosa's cell phone beeped. "Sorry. I told Eddie where I'd be. He was checking on Detective Dill." She took the call, then turned to Cristina. "That was Eddie. Detective Dill wasn't at work yesterday. In fact he has taken indefinite leave of absence."

"So he was in Santa Fe," Cristina said and drew closer to her friend. Rosa wasn't just imagining things. Someone *had* tried to kill her.

CHAPTER TWENTY-ONE

"What did Cristina say?" Eddie asked, washing down the moo-shu beef pancakes with a Tsingtao beer. They were having lunch at Tso Garden, Rosa's favorite Chinese restaurant on Valley Boulevard, waiting for Eddie's contact in the LAPD to show up. Rosa was only picking at her hot garlic chicken.

"Same thing you said, 'I'm too caught up in this thing.' I need to rest. Damn, I haven't even graded my last set of papers. I haven't prepared for classes. I've dropped everything..."

She paused and looked at Eddie, afraid her voice would break. He reached across and held her hands.

"Hey, you can pull through. What I worry about is that these people have your number. If Dill was not in L.A. yesterday, then he could've been in Santa Fe—"

"Trying to run me over," Rosa completed his thought.

"What I can't understand is how these three men are connected. I mean, Malorio, El Jefe, and Dill. It just doesn't make sense."

"Maybe your friend will know." Rosa nodded toward the young Chicano detective walking in the door.

She recognized Roberto Mejía, Bobby to his friends. They had met briefly at one of Eddie's productions. Handsome, young, a smart dresser, he turned the heads of women as he walked into the restaurant. And single. He had asked Rosa for a date during intermission, but at the time she was too busy with classes to accept.

There was an air of confidence about him, an aura of trustworthiness. It was obvious he was street smart. He nodded at a couple of locals in a booth near the door. He knew the place, and by his presence he made it his turf. He was also the only cop who attended plays at the barrio theater.

Better looking than Jimmy Smits, thought Rosa. I should have said yes to his offer.

Eddie and Bobby greeted each other with a barrio handshake. "Hey, homes, good to see you. You remember Rosa."

"I sure do. We met at the theater. Cal State profe, right. And the ChupaCabra detective." He smiled and held out his hand. "Hi, Rosa."

"Cal State profe if I can keep my job," Rosa answered without smiling, "but *not* the ChupaCabra detective."

"Sorry," Bobby apologized. "You are in the news—"

"Which is why we need to talk to you," Eddie said. "Sit down, join us for lunch."

"Thanks, just coffee," he said to the waiter. "So, how's the new play coming? Got a part for me?"

"Play's coming along fine, and I'll put you on stage any time you're ready."

"I have no talent," he said and winked at Rosa. "So, how can I help?"

"What do you know about Chuco's autopsy?" Rosa asked.

Bobby glanced around the room, then leaned forward. "The death has the medical investigator puzzled. What kind of machine can destroy a man's brains? They think it's some kind of pump—"

"You think it was done with a machine?" Rosa interrupted.

Bobby leaned back. "What else? Look, I'll be up front. I'm not a ChupaCabra believer. If that means I can't help you, then I'm sorry."

"No, no," Eddie cut in. "You can help. Listen to Rosa's story."

"Sure." Bobby nodded and sipped his coffee. *Show me* he seemed to say. His attitude softened after Rosa finished relating what had happened to her since José's death.

"Damn, you've been through a lot." His eyes told her he believed her. "What can I do?"

"We can't get any information on the two men in México," Eddie said, "but we thought you could enlighten us about Dill."

Bobby frowned slightly. "You know I can't discuss personnel."

"Rosa's in danger!" Eddie said, raising his voice. "All we want is help."

Bobby nodded. "This is between the three of us, right?"

"Like blood," Eddie replied. Rosa nodded.

"There's an internal investigation going on. Involves drugs."

"There's police involved," Eddie said. He had immediately made the connection.

Bobby shrugged. "It smells really bad. Could blow the roof off LAPD—much worse than the Rodney King case. It could involve cops on the take. That's it."

"Let's assume you don't believe Dill tried to run me down," Rosa continued. "I can understand that. But what if he was there? Why?"

"*If* he was there, it doesn't make sense. Unless it has some-thing to do with your visit to the crack house. You found the get-away tunnel the cops should have found. The chief really came down hard on the entire precinct."

"Dill's on leave," Eddie said.

Bobby nodded.

"What about the break-in at my apartment?"

"I checked into it, like Eddie asked. No prints. The officer in charge wrote it off as kids looking for something to steal for drug money."

"But nothing was taken."

"Yeah. Maybe you have something they want."

"What?" Eddie asked.

"I have no idea," Rosa replied.

Bobby stood. "Look, I'll keep my eyes open. You quit playing investigator," he said to Rosa. "Don't you have students' papers to grade?"

Rosa took the jab with a smile. "It's spring break, Bobby."

He took her hand and whispered. "Just be careful. See you at the play, Eddie."

"Thanks, homes. Thanks a lot."

He turned and they watched him walk away.

"Nice, but a little arrogant," Rosa said.

"He's okay. Being a Chicano cop isn't easy. Apparently the internal investigation he mentioned has the whole department concerned. Something big is coming down."

Rosa's phone buzzed and she answered.

"It's me, Rosa. Alfredo. It's happened again, it's happened again." He was crying.

Rosa tensed. "Que pasó?"

"Herminio. He's dead. They murdered Herminio. The village is empty. The people are leaving. Can you come, Rosa? Lupe needs you. Can you come?"

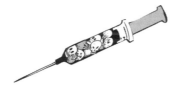

CHAPTER TWENTY-TWO

"No way you're going!" Eddie insisted. "I won't let you. It's too dangerous."

"Eddie, I have to. Herminio's dead. I have to go—for Lupe's sake."

She knew he was worried, but she knew she had to return to Lago Negro. Herminio had been a trusted friend; now she had to be there for Lupe.

"Call Cristina, please. I bet she'll tell you the same thing."

"I know, Eddie, and I'd appreciate her concern as much as yours. But I have to go."

Eddie gave in reluctantly. "All right. But I don't like it. I feel something bad is—"

"I'll be careful," Rosa said, leaning to kiss his cheek. "And I'll be back in time for the play."

Eddie smiled. "I want you there opening night."

"I'll be there. Promise. Now, if you'll drop me at my place I'll pick up a few things and head out to the airport. I'll take my car—"

"You sure?"

"It's faster and you're busy," Rosa replied.

Eddie drove her to her apartment, then with a warm embrace and a warning for her be careful he waved and drove away.

Rosa entered her apartment with trepidation. She felt something in her had been violated by the person who broke in and went through her things. True, nothing was taken, but the thief *had* taken away something: a knowledge of her private world. She would much rather have lost all her possessions than to feel that a stranger out there knew intimate things about her.

She called the airline and reserved an afternoon flight to Puerto Vallarta. Then she packed underclothes, toiletries, a pair of jeans and blouse, and her small digital camera. Her light leather jacket was all she needed. She remembered the knife Father Larry had given her, and she slipped it into the bag, without thinking if it would clear security.

As she was packing she thought about what Bobby had said. Whoever broke in was looking for something, and only Rosa knew what it was.

She walked around the apartment, noting every single thing that might have value. But it wasn't monetary value the thief was after. It was something else.

Her books? She ran her hands along the book shelf. No. Her papers? They were scattered on her small desk. No, not the papers.

What then? Painfully, her mind retraced the events that had occurred the night José was killed. A series of images ran through her mind. Flashes of people, places, smells and sounds, the clearing in the jungle. Her mind briefly weighed each image for its importance, until she saw herself the morning she found José.

She had tripped on something. José's large camera—bigger than her cheap digital one because José was learning documentary photography the old-fashioned way. It was lying on the ground. She had picked it up. He had taken pictures that night!

She had brought the camera back in his backpack! It was still in the trunk of her car!

Breathlessly she hurried out to her car and opened the trunk. There it was! The thief who broke into her apartment had been looking for the camera!

She looked at her watch. No time to call anyone. She got her bag and drove down Whittier until she spotted a camera shop. She stopped and rushed in with the camera in hand.

"There's film in this camera!" she exclaimed to the pimply-faced young man who sat reading a lowrider magazine. "Can you develop it?"

"Yeah, lady, that's what we do. Why don't you take it out of the camera?"

"Oh, yes." Rosa realized her hands were trembling.

"Can you do it?" she asked the young man.

"Nice camera," he said as he took out the roll of film. "Wanna sell it? I can get you good money."

"No. I'm in a hurry," Rosa muttered. "Just develop the film."

He tossed the roll in the air and caught it. "We're busy, but I could rush it a little . . ." He tossed the roll in the air again. It came down in slow motion, like a bomb about to explode with its dark secret.

"Yes. Rush it. Please." Rosa understood what he needed. She reached into her purse, took out a twenty and shoved it into his hands. "Please."

"Orale!" He smiled and disappeared.

Damn! Rosa cursed. Did I do the right thing? Can I trust him? Should I have called Eddie? Should I call Cristina? She looked at her watch. No time.

She paused and took a deep breath. Por el amor de Dios, Rosa, get hold of yourself. You don't need to call anyone to develop film. This is their business. Everything was going to be all right.

She was alone in the shop. The clock on the wall stared down at her. Time seemed to slow down. The second hand barely moved. She could hear it ticking as it crept around the numbers, threatening to stop at any moment.

Please hurry, Rosa thought. She glanced at the well-thumbed magazines on the table next to her. Then back at the clock. Why was the clock slowing down? Was she having a panic attack? She felt warm. Was she going to be sick?

Nervously she got up and looked out the window at the traffic. A police car passed by and Rosa drew back. Was that Detective Dill in the car? No, she told herself. No, no, no! I'm imagining things.

"Laaaay-dy!" Someone called behind her, and Rosa jumped. She spun around ready to defend herself. "God," she gasped.

"Hey, sorry," the clerk apologized. He had appeared out of nowhere. "Here's your film. Record time, huh." He smiled and handed her the envelope.

"Yes, good," Rosa replied, taking the envelope and tearing it open. She flipped through the photographs José had taken.

José had taken many photos of a helicopter in the jungle clearing. What was a helicopter doing there? She looked closely. Two men were carrying bags. She could see their faces. What in the hell were they doing landing in the jungle where the ChupaCabra had killed the goats?

When she flipped to the last photo her blood froze. The figure in the photo seemed to be rushing at the camera. José had captured the ChupaCabra on film!

Rosa gasped. The image was terrifying. It was the beast that killed José!

"Dear God," she whispered.

"Hey, lady, you okay?" the clerk asked. He had seen Rosa go pale when she looked at the film. "Can I get you some water or something?"

Rosa shook her head. No, there was nothing he could do. She stuffed the photographs in the envelope and hurried out the door to her car.

CHAPTER TWENTY-THREE

Alfredo was waiting for Rosa in the Puerto Vallarta terminal.

"Dios, I can't believe it," she whispered. "I am so sorry, Alfredo."

"It's terrible, terrible," he replied. "Herminio was like a father to me." He picked up her bag and led her to his car. "I am glad you could come. When I told Lupe you were coming she felt relief. It has been very difficult for her. But you look tired. Are you all right?"

"I am tired, y muy triste," Rosa admitted.

She had gone to the lavatory just before the plane landed, and what she saw in the mirror surprised her. Her face was pale and drawn, her eyes dark with fatigue. Seeing the image of the ChupaCabra in the photograph had shocked her, and she knew she would *not* be able to show the photo to anyone. The image was too horrible.

"I borrowed my cousin's car," Alfredo explained as he opened the door for her. He placed her bag in the backseat.

"How is Lupe?"

"She's a strong woman, but she is very sad. She and Herminio were happy together. Her family was with her at the burial this morning—"

"So quick?"

"Sí. Es costumbre."

Rosa sighed. "Tell me what happened."

"He had an argument with El Jefe. Herminio couldn't stand to see the people being driven from the village. He held a meeting with the villagers and told them they had to stand up to El Jefe. Then El Jefe showed up and threatened Herminio. That night Herminio was killed. Someone attacked him. He was brutally beaten."

Alfredo paused. Even recounting the event was difficult. Herminio had been a strong leader in the village. With his death the campesinos were ready to pack their meager belongings and leave.

"El Jefe spread the rumor that the ChupaCabra had killed him, but I know it was Jefe's men."

"And the police?"

"They do nothing. Estan comprados."

Rosa handed him the photographs Jose had taken of the helicopter. "José took these photos the night he was killed."

"A helicopter? Are the men unloading packages? I don't understand."

"Someone is using that clearing in the jungle to land helicopters—"

"Ah," Alfredo exclaimed, "that explains the noises people heard at night. But why?"

"I suspect it's a drop point for drugs."

"Of course!" Alfredo hit the steering wheel with the palm of his hand. "It makes sense. They need to get rid of the villagers to carry on their clandestine operation. And El Jefe is behind the whole operation! But the photos are incriminating. I can clearly see El Jefe and other men. You need to show it to the police."

"Can we trust the police?" Rosa asked.

Alfredo shook his head. "What can we do?"

"We go into the jungle tonight," Rosa said.

"But—" Alfredo hesitated. "That can be very dangerous. These men will do anything to protect themselves, and their business."

"I have to verify what José saw."

Alfredo nodded. To revenge Hermino's death he was ready to do anything.

"But what do you expect to find? The photos don't explain the way José died."

Rosa understood. But she dared not show him the ChupaCabra photo. Not now, maybe never.

Alfredo pulled up in front of Lupe's home. The bright southern sun beat down on the deserted streets and homes of the once lively village. Lupe, dressed in black, came out to greet them.

She cried when Rosa embraced her. "Ay, Rosa, I'm so glad to see you. Such a horrible thing happened to my Herminio. Why should he die in such a way? He never harmed anyone."

"I know, Lupe. It's a terrible tragedy. I am so sorry. What can I do?"

"Ay, Rosa, you are too kind. You will always have a home here. What am I saying? There is no home. The people are leaving Lago Negro. One by one they go. This is a village of fear. I, too, must leave the place of my birth."

She explained that her brother was coming for her. Her family did not want her to be alone. A curse hung over the village, the curse of the ChupaCabra.

The village women had brought food for the wake, but there was little festivity. Friends and neighbors arrived to give their condolences and left quietly. The village was nearly deserted.

Rosa sat with Lupe through the afternoon. Lupe talked about her life with Herminio. Although they had no children, they had shared a full and happy life. At dusk her brother and his wife arrived and she said goodbye to the home she had known with Herminio.

"Don't stay," she warned Rosa. "Come with us. Don't stay in Lago Negro."

"I'll be safe. Alfredo is with me. I plan to stay in Puerto tonight and return home tomorrow." She lied. She could not tell Lupe that she planned to be watching for helicopters, nor that she had helped herself to some of the funeral food to eat with Alfredo in the selva.

"Don't worry, señora, I will take care of her," Alfredo promised.

Rosa sighed. "I only wish there was something more I could do."

"You have done me good by being here," Lupe replied. "Thank you for coming. I know Herminio is happy you came to share this time with me. He was a brave man. He stood up against the evil men. But they have won. Nothing is left."

"They won't win," Rosa said. "I promise you. I will phone you. And this summer I will come and visit."

"Yes, come. Adios, Rosa. Cuidate. There is much evil in the world."

She kissed Rosa goodbye, then got in her brother's car. The car chugged away, down the dusty road toward the Puerto Vallarta highway.

Rosa turned to Alfredo. "Are you ready?"

"Listo," he replied. He picked up Rosa's backpack and they headed into the jungle. "But will they come tonight?"

"I don't know," Rosa said.

It was dark when they found the clearing where José had been murdered. Rosa pointed to palmettos where they could hide and wait. From there they could watch for the arrival of the helicopter, or the ChupaCabra.

Around them the jungle settled into darkness. Birds called, iguanas scurried in the trees, and mosquitoes swarmed. A bullfrog bellowed in the dark, and as if in answer, the foghorn of a cruise ship sounded far away. From where they sat they couldn't see the ocean.

Rosa opened her backpack, took out sandwiches and candy. They ate in silence. She checked her digital camera. She didn't dare use the flash, so she didn't know if photos would take.

It was after midnight when they heard the drone overhead, distant at first, then descending over them like an extraterrestrial from the dark sky. Its blinding lights probed the dense jungle, illuminating the clearing before it descended. Like a demon come to claim its territory, the helicopter landed.

Beside her she heard Alfredo curse. "Chingao. I don't believe it."

They waited breathlessly as the pilot cut the power and two men jumped out. Working fast they unloaded bags, tossing them on the ground. They spoke little, glanced around from time to time, and when they were done they got into the helicopter, and soon the chopper was airborne. It zoomed into the sky and disappeared.

"You were right," Alfredo whispered. "Drogas."

"Let's check," Rosa replied. She took her flashlight and the knife Father Larry had given her and hurried to the bags. She cut a hole in one of the bags and shone her light on the white powder that spilled out.

"Cocaina!" Alfredo gasped. "A big load."

"There's more," Rosa said, shining the light on a bag labeled Medical Supplies: pseudoephedrine. The key ingredient for cooking meth. "Probably from Asia, or labs in Mexico City."

Alfredo cursed again. "These packages must be worth millions to the dealers. And they bring it here. Why? Where does it go?"

The sound of a truck chugging up the path from Lago Negro cut him short. They ran back to their hiding place. They watched as a delivery truck drove up to the bags containing the drugs. A sign on the side of the truck read, Frutas de Puerto Vallarta, Felix Brothers S.A.

Two men stepped into the lights of the truck. One called to his partner. "Esos hijos de la chingada were early tonight. Anda, load up!"

"Malorio," Rosa whispered. The so-called keeper of the ChupaCabra was a dope smuggler.

The two worked quickly and loaded the bags into the truck.

"Que mas?" Malorio's crony asked when they were done.

"Nada mas," Malorio replied. "We have the ChupaCabra, y la carga."

As he spoke a horrifying scream exploded from inside the truck.

"Ese pinche animal es el diablo," the man said. "Why take it with you? Why not kill it? It is evil."

"Kill my pet? Oh no." Malorio laughed. "I take the ChupaCabra to the states. I let it loose in Los Angeles and soon everyone will beg for mercy."

"I don't like it," the man said. "It is the devil. And you are the devil's helper if you turn it loose. I wish I had never gotten into this bad business."

Malorio shrugged and took a pistol from his belt. "Pues, it is easy to get out of the business, amigo."

The man cried "No!" and held up his hands just as Malorio fired. The man stumbled forward, cursed Malorio, and caught a second bullet in the chest.

The explosions startled birds in the trees, and a raucous flapping filled the air. Another horrifying scream sounded inside the truck. Malorio laughed.

"ChupaCabra, my pet. Let us sail to Los Angeles. There you will walk the streets with those hijos de la chingada!"

His curse echoed in the dark as he got in the truck and drove away.

"He . . . he killed the man," Alfredo gasped.

"There's nothing we can do," Rosa said. "Vamos!" She grabbed Alfredo's arm and they stumbled out of the jungle back to the car that Alfredo had hidden behind Herminio's home.

"What now?" Alfredo asked.

"Try to find him," Rosa replied.

As the first rose-colored light of dawn filled the eastern sky, they drove into the city.

"There are too many places for him to hide," Alfredo said. "And if he took the highway north we cannot catch him."

"Yes," Rosa agreed. "Unless they don't use trucks."

"Then by plane or ship," Alfredo suggested.

"He said *sail to Los Angeles*. Is that what you heard?"

"Yes!"

"Let's try the port!" Rosa exclaimed. "Maybe they use motorboats to transport the drugs north."

As Alfredo drove along the waterfront toward the cruise ships, the sun rose, bathing the city and the bay in glorious light.

"There!" Rosa cried.

Stationed near *Destiny*, a medium-sized Celebration Lines cruise ship, sat Malorio's truck.

"The ship was here overnight," Alfredo said. "It sails for L.A. this morning."

"That's where Malorio said the drugs were headed! They're using the cruise ship to transport the drugs!"

CHAPTER TWENTY-FOUR

The men at the truck worked swiftly, loading the packages of drugs through the ship's cargo door. A customs official stood nearby, but he looked the other way. As far as anyone observing the process was concerned the Felix Brothers had just loaded fresh fruit aboard the cruise ship. When the loading was done a man drove the truck away.

"What now?" Alfredo asked.

"I'm going to see if I can purchase a ticket for the return trip," Rosa said.

"Rosa, wait. I think it best we report what we saw to the police."

"Won't do any good," Rosa replied, "you know that."

"Yes, you're right," Alfredo agreed. "But to return with the ship would be dangerous. Someone might recognize you."

"That's a chance I have to take," Rosa said. "Wait here."

In the city throngs of hard working Mexicans went about their business, filling the streets as they went to work. Buses clanged toward the Centro, cars wove in and out of the zocalo.

The workers of the city were unaware of the cargo the pleasure ship now held in its belly.

Rosa walked into the terminal nearest the cruise ship, and a man sweeping the floor pointed her in the direction of the ticket office. There, a sleepy-eyed, stocky man was just opening the door.

"Buenos dias," Rosa greeted him. "I want to buy a ticket on the ship returning to Los Angeles."

The agent looked her over and frowned. He glanced at her wet and muddy shoes. Ah, the Americanas had no taste, his look said. Just another norteamericana in jeans who had been out all night having a good time.

"Did you come with the ship?"

"No."

"But it sails in an hour." He shrugged his shoulders and turned away, dismissing her.

"But I'm ready to board. All I need is a ticket."

He looked at her. "How did you get here?"

"I flew."

"So you want to return with the ship?"

"Yes."

"Are you American?"

"Yes. I'm a Chicana from the USA."

"Ah, Chicana. Doesn't that mean pocha?" He grinned.

"No, it means liberated."

Her response startled the agent. He appreciated her spunk. "Do you have a passport?" he asked.

Rosa dug through her wallet and handed him her passport.

He looked at it carefully. "A Mexican Americana, huh. Your parents went to el norte?"

"Long ago," Rosa said.

"I have relatives that went to Los Angeles. They say life is difficult there."

"Yes," Rosa agreed. "Borders separate people."

"I read the papers," the agent said. "They like for Mexicans to do the work, but not to live there. It doesn't make sense. Well, how will you pay for the boleto?"

Rosa took her credit card from her wallet.

He shook his head. "I am sorry, señorita, but the round-trip ticket must be purchased in Los Angeles. I cannot sell you only a one-way ticket."

"Are there rooms available?" Rosa asked.

"Yes. As a matter of fact, this is a new cruise, definitely not sold out. There are many rooms in the lower deck."

Rosa reached into her wallet and drew out a twenty, which she slipped across to him. "I am sure someone like you who has a great responsibility to the cruise line can book me passage."

The ticket agent cleared his throat. "Well, since there are rooms available...And you do have a valid passport..."

"Certified," Rosa said and smiled.

He slipped the money in his pocket and returned her smile. "Yes, certified Chicana."

Methodically he set about issuing her a ticket. When he was done Rosa thanked him.

"I have issued you a boarding pass. You have to board immediately," the agent said. "Go to the purser's office to get room and meal assignment. There should be no trouble."

Again Rosa thanked him and hurried out.

"I got it," she told Alfredo who was waiting by the car. "So we part company. Thank you for everything, Alfredo."

"De nada." He shrugged. "I wish I could do more to bring Malorio and his gang to justice. But I don't like what you're doing. These people stop at nothing. Cuidate."

Rosa nodded. She understood the danger, but following the shipment was the only way to identify Malorio as the man transporting the drugs. When the ship docked in L.A. she would grab the nearest customs agent or policeman. Sending Malorio to prison would fulfill the promise she had made.

"I'll be careful, amigo," Rosa promised, embracing him. She took her bag and walked quickly toward the gangplank.

A tall, blonde ship officer gave her the once over as she handed him her boarding pass. Many of the passengers had partied in the city, but all had returned in the early morning hours. Here was someone he couldn't quite place.

"Out late?" he inquired.

She looked down at her wrinkled jeans and muddy shoes. "We went for a walk on the beach. I haven't had time to change."

"Understandable," he said and waved her aboard. Rosa headed for the purser's office for her room key and meal ticket.

"You didn't come down with us?" asked the purser, a young woman with a British accent. "The agent issued you a ticket?"

"My uncle works for the cruise line," Rosa lied.

"I see. Okay, welcome aboard. You're all alone on the lower deck, aft. Here's a map of the ship. Breakfast is just starting, and we cast anchor in an hour. Have fun, dearie."

"Thanks," Rosa replied. "Easier than I thought," she said to herself as she made her way to her cabin.

On the main deck she ran into passengers going to breakfast. She skirted them and at midship she took a flight of stairs down. She had just turned into the dimly lighted hallway when two figures made her freeze. She quietly withdrew around the corner.

She was just a few feet away from Frank Dill, the LAPD detective, and El Jefe.

"I'm telling you, it went without a hitch! You damn Mexicans worry about everything!" Dill grumbled.

"Yes, but you lost track of the girl!" El Jefe replied angrily.

"So what? She means nothing to us. Soon as we reach L.A. we collect. We're rich, Jefe! Rich!"

"You may be done when we deliver, but for me this is my business. This operation is good for millions. You Americanos are too easily satisfied. Me, I want more."

Dill laughed. "Yeah, well count me in. This is the easiest score I ever made."

"Thanks to me," Jefe replied. "There's still work to do. Check the cargo. Make sure everything is in place. I don't trust Dago. Young kids can't be trusted. They smell the money and they get ideas. Your job is to keep him in line."

"And you?"

"I'm going to see if this pinche cruise ship serves tacos con salsa picante."

"What about Malorio?" Dill asked.

"As long as he takes care of ChupaCabra he's okay. After that, adios." With one hand he made a slicing motion at his throat.

Both laughed, and parted. As Dill walked down the hall, Rosa sucked in her breath and pressed against the wall; he went past her corridor without seeing her.

Rosa felt the ship lurch slightly. It was pulling away from the dock. They were on their way to L.A. She drew a deep breath and followed Dill.

CHAPTER TWENTY-FIVE

Dill slouched down the hallway and disappeared through a door marked *Ship Personnel Only*. Should I follow? thought Rosa. Yes, that's why I'm here.

Cautiously Rosa opened the door, stepped over the threshold, and descended a flight of stairs into the cargo area. The dark hold was stocked high with crates.

Rosa moved carefully through the labyrinth of crates. She could feel the ship moving. While the cruise passengers gathered on the upper decks to have their morning coffee and wave good-bye to Puerto Vallarta, Rosa found herself in the cargo compartment of the ship, following a policeman who had gone rotten.

Dill and El Jefe, and whoever else worked with them, had made a deal with the narcotraficantes. A deal worth millions. If Dill found Rosa, he would kill her to silence her. And only Alfredo knew she was on board. She could easily be dumped at sea—a meal for sharks. And Alfredo didn't know Dill and Jefe were aboard ship, so Rosa's disappearance could not implicate them.

She heard voices ahead and edged forward, passing huge plastic containers of diesel fuel. Two figures stood at a steel table, illuminated by a light hanging over the table. She recognized Dill's voice. Drawing closer, she peered around a crate.

"Do as I say, Dago," Dill told the young man, "and you'll do all right. Fuck up and you'll never work again."

"I know what I'm supposed to do," Dago replied, "but this place gives me the creeps. The whole place is fucking creepy."

"Has Malorio been around?" Dill asked.

"Yeah, he was here. He goes back there, sniffs around, then he disappears." He motioned over his shoulder. "What's he got in the cage? A monkey?"

"Yeah, a big ape. You keep away from there," Dill cautioned. "That's Malorio's baby. All you have to do is make sure no one snoops around our stuff. You got the captain's orders?"

"Yeah, yeah," Dago replied. "No one comes in this area." He held up a piece of paper then tossed it on the table. The paper landed on top of a deck of playing cards spread out in a game of solitaire. Beside the cards lay a pistol.

"Good," Dill said. "Any nosy crewman comes snooping, you make sure they keep the hell out. We're two days from scoring, so we don't want anything to go wrong."

"Don't worry, the dope's safe—"

Dill reached forward and grabbed Dago by the collar. "Shut up! Don't mention the word, you hear! As far as you're concerned we've got this area restricted because we're delivering a dangerous ape to L.A.! Is that clear!"

He pushed Dago aside.

"Yeah, yeah, it's clear. An ape. Everyone knows there aren't fucking apes in Mexico."

"You talk too much, Dago. You keep that up and you won't last. Just keep your mouth shut. I'll be back soon as I find Malo."

"Yeah, I'll keep my trap shut," Dago said in parting. "It's spooky, that's all."

"You're getting paid well," Dill called, and passed a few feet from Rosa on his way out.

"Yeah, well, screw the money," Dago muttered to himself. He turned to the table and his card game, picked up the Glock special, and checked the clip. "All I know is I'm not going to sleep till we get to L.A.," he mumbled.

The light shone on Dago's face, and Rosa read fear in the young man's eyes. Not fear of Dill, but of Malorio's beast. An ape in a crate? No, not an ape, but ChupaCabra, the beast on its way to L.A. on board a ship full of innocent passengers.

Rosa turned and quietly slipped around the stacks of cartons to the back of the hold. Her eyes, now accustomed to the dark, could read the labels on the crates. Felix Brothers, fruta. Inside were the bags of dope.

In the 1960s and 1970s even governments had found the drug trade a source of revenue. Those wishing to overthrow the Sandinistas in Nicaragua had sold drugs to raise money for their so-called anti-communist cause. Now the narcrotraficantes continued to feed the market, making fortunes as they hooked the sons and daughters of a new generation.

But big business required a new technology, thought Rosa. Sophisticated computers, jet planes, high speed boats, moles inside police departments, distribution systems, and if need be, a cruise ship DEA and customs wouldn't suspect.

She sought the exit, but in the dark the maze of crates confused her. She lost her way.

She continued forward, feeling her way by touching the sides of the crates. Suddenly a bad odor reached her nostrils—something she had smelled before. What was it? Sulfur, a horrible stench. Then a shuffling sound, as if something was dragging itself along the floor.

"Virgen María," Rosa whispered.

A noise like the whining of a dog broke the silence. Whatever had followed her in the dark was right behind her!

She turned and peered into the dark. Something large and hairy moved between the crates of dope. Two red eyes were watching her every move.

She stifled a cry. Malorio? No, something else. The beast in the photo!

Rosa felt a surge of adrenalin. An instinctive, primitive energy coursed through her body. Something told her this is how her ancestors must have felt a million years ago when they encountered a dangerous predator in the jungle.

She crouched and reached for her knife. She was ready to fight for her life. Whatever monster lay in the dark depths might kill her, but she would go down slashing and fighting.

Again the creature moved. It had smelled her! Its burning eyes were the eyes of death. It hurled itself at Rosa only to crash against the bars of the cage that held it captive.

It grunted and moved back into the recesses of the cage, enclosing itself in a kind of cloak, or leathery wings.

Rosa stepped back, her heart pounding. In the dark she hadn't seen the cage bars. She backed away slowly, trembling, suddenly aware of all the pieces in the puzzle.

ChupaCabra was destined for L.A. Like coke and meth, it would be set loose in the streets to destroy people. Crank, crystals, meth, the ChupaCabra, by whatever name, these were the brainsuckers of the young and vulnerable.

Rosa found the door, slipped out of the dark hold, and up a stairway. Cautiously she made her way toward her room, her trembling legs barely able to carry her.

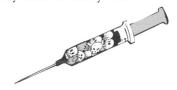

CHAPTER TWENTY-SIX

An exhausted Rosa opened the door to her stateroom and stumbled in. Now she knew: the ChupaCabra was part of the shipment of illicit drugs. Mind destroyers on course for el norte, specifically the port of L.A.

She threw her carry-on bag on one of the beds and looked out the window. The port of Puerto Vallarta had already disappeared. They were on the open sea, and the ship was moving fast. They would sail all day and all night. Now that she knew where the drugs were hidden, she had to lay low until they arrived in L.A., then expose the traffickers.

She stripped and stepped into the shower. The hot water and fresh scent of the soap helped ease her weariness. She said a silent prayer to the Virgen de Guadalupe. I hope I haven't bitten off more than I can chew, she thought. She stood for a long time under the stinging hot water, washing away the sweat and grime that clung to her body.

"Malorio's ape," she said to herself. In the 1950s to have a monkey on your back meant to be hooked on heroin. Now those hooked on drugs had the ChupaCabra on their backs.

The cocaine was for those with money; the meth could be processed almost anywhere. Crystals to burn brains with. Meth cooked in the secrecy of kitchens across the country. Recipes on the Internet. An entire generation was being enslaved while governments in power paid lip service to the devastation.

She dried herself briskly and slipped into her pajamas. She had brought a toothbrush and toothpaste, and a change of clothes. That's all she needed. And a good sleep.

She crawled under the covers and closed her eyes. Beneath her she felt the movement of the ship as it sliced through the waves with hardly an effort. The forward motion created a lulling effect. She had been aboard a ship once before; as students, she and Cristina had taken a cruise to Seattle during spring break.

So long ago! Ah, undergraduate life seemed so unencumbered. They worried about papers and grades. They joined MECHA and picketed the stores that sold non-union grapes. One week they drove to Sacramento and joined a César Chávez sit-in. Conservative politicians responded by saying "we're against quotas," thus killing the educational chances of so many people of color.

Now, as she thought about those times, Rosa realized how innocent they seemed. Of course she and her friends were serious in their intent. They were idealistic and they argued long and hard about a democratic society and the rights of minority groups. Never could she have imagined finding herself in this predicament, on a ship with millions of dollars worth of drugs in its hold, along with a terrifying beast.

She tossed restlessly. She had lost friends, José and Chuco and Herminio. She wanted to have the time to pray for them, to grieve for them, but her life had been on a roller coaster since José's death.

With these thoughts she slipped into a world of dreams. The images were disturbing at first. She saw helicopters in the air, dozens of them hovering like unearthly creatures over the jungles and forests of the south. Loaded with drugs they spread across the world and deposited their deadly cargo on school grounds where innocent children played.

She saw men and women working as slaves, hoeing rows of poppies, collecting the milk of the ripened flowers. Some carried heavy bags filled with cocaine, which they dumped into trucks that roared across the country, raising whirlwinds of despair in their wake.

A demon rose from the emaciated bodies of the workers, a beast rising from the piles of drugs. With vicious claws and bloody fangs, it crushed the young beneath its cloven feet. ChupaCabra, the brainsucker, rose like a specter in Rosa's path.

She heard herself scream, she ran, fell. Just as the leathery wings swept over her, voices lifted her to safety. Indio and Uncle Billy called her name and pulled her into a hogan. She entered and saw a sandpainting on the floor, exquisite earth colors depicting corn plants and the figures of ancestral spirits. Symbols she didn't understand, but which eased her anxiety. In the hogan where Uncle Billy performed his ceremony the evil of the ChupaCabra could not enter.

She saw the cross she had given Uncle Billy. It lay on the sandpainting. They were praying over it and thus sending her protection. Uncle Billy pulled her forward and told her to sit on the sandpainting. Realizing the ceremony was for her, she did as instructed.

Uncle Billy began his chant, a song that had been passed down to the singers across the generations. This was one of the many chants that told the stories of the ancestral spirits. It was to make Rosa well, to integrate her soul, to give her power over the ChupaCabra.

For a long time Rosa sat in the middle of the hogan, listening to the chant, feeling the energy of the people around her. The many voices singing lulled her into a deep sleep, and there her body and soul rested and renewed themselves.

When it was time to return to the real world Uncle Billy spoke, telling her the evil of the sorcerers still lurked outside the hogan. Evil surrounded the world, but now she was strong enough to fight back. Fight back for the people.

Uncle Billy intoned: "Those who follow the ways of the ancestors can fight the dope pushers who blow witch objects into the body. I will pull the witch objects out of your soul. You will become a warrior woman. You are in harmony with nature and your community. You are a warrior for the people."

Rosa smiled and thanked the old man. She thanked Indio who was learning the chant. This young man who had once gotten lost in the world of drugs and had once been frightened by Skinwalkers was now in charge of his destiny. He would become a singer and help his people.

There was a way out of the darkness. One could learn to fight the drug obsession. Both body and soul could be saved. For Indio the way lay in the path of his ancestors. So too for the young people Rosa tutored at the clinic. Their ancestors had given them a good path to follow, if they could only find it.

There were many ways to learn the path. Listen to the stories and history of the ancestors. Learn to know yourself, as the ancient Greeks taught. Know your soul. Live in harmony with nature and neighbors as her ancestors had taught. Know your community and become a warrior. The road was open to everyone.

The dream was a revelation. The vision of hope belonged to all. Rosa had worked her way beyond the images of destruction to the centering in the hogan, the healing power of the sandpainting, the songs of Uncle Billy.

She smiled and fell further into a very peaceful sleep.

When she awakened she glanced at her watch. She had slept all day and into the night. Just as well, she thought. I have nothing to do until we reach L.A. But you do have to eat, her groaning stomach told her.

She rose and slipped into her clean jeans, sweater and light jacket. She would carry only her wallet, phone, and the knife in her jacket.

Have to chance it and go in search of food, she thought. Knowing that Dill, Jefe, and Malorio were aboard ship gave her the upper hand. She could watch out for them.

She was about to open the door of her stateroom when an unpleasant odor caught her attention. It was the smell of sulphur just outside her room.

A scratching at the doorknob made Rosa jump. Whoever or whatever was outside wanted in. Only the deadbolt kept the door from opening. Rosa glanced at the porthole. There was no way to break the small windows, and even if she could she could only drop into the ocean and drown. She had to stand and fight. Breathless, she waited. She could hear the churning of the ship's motor, the giant propellers turning in the dark sea.

Then the scratching noises stopped; whatever had been outside her door was gone. Rosa breathed a sigh of relief.

But what was it? Could it have been only a steward come to turn down her bed? Was her imagination running away with her?

Surely Dill, Jefe, and Malorio didn't know she was aboard ship?

Cautiously, she opened the door and peered down the hall. All was quiet. She sniffed the air. There was no doubt, the terrible odor of the ChupaCabra lingered in the air. Or was it the smell of fear? Her own fear. Had she really seen the doorknob turn?

Someone knows I'm here, she thought, as she sprinted down the hallway.

CHAPTER TWENTY-SEVEN

At the end of the hall, Rosa found a flight of stairs that led to the upper decks. She didn't stop running until she breathed fresh air.

The deck was empty. Those passengers who had finished dinner were probably at the casino or at the nightly entertainment. Somewhere she had seen the poster announcing the show, a musical called *Yankee Doodle*.

Overhead the night sky was full of stars; the sea was calm, rocking the ship so softly the motion was barely noticeable. For a few moments the inscrutable presence of the sea touched Rosa, and she gathered her strength.

Her survival instinct kicked in and she reviewed what she had found out. Dill had said the captain had been paid off, and that meant there was no way to get a message to L.A. What if Dill had checked the passenger list and found out she was on board? They would be looking for her.

Someone appeared on the deck and Rosa drew back into the shadows. An elderly couple strode by, then stood at the rail, arm in arm, enjoying the night air, shunning the smoke-filled, noisy casino and *Yankee Doodle*.

Was there anyone on board ship she could trust, Rosa wondered. The answer was no. By taking a room, she had advertised she was on board. She would have to be extremely cautious.

Hunger drove her up the stairs to the snack bar on the topmost deck. The place was deserted. She moved cautiously and grabbed three sandwiches and a bottle of orange juice, then withdrew into the shadows to eat.

Savagely, she tore away the cellophane wrapping and ate in a hurry, swallowing the chunks of cheese and meat, constantly sweeping the area for signs of danger. She drank down the orange juice in huge gulps. Then she paused to sniff the air, as if by smelling she could detect the enemy before it found her.

"Stay calm, mujer," she told herself. "You're acting like an animal."

She was surprised by how sharp her instincts had become. Something primitive had surfaced when she saw ChupaCabra. She had wanted to strike out with the knife, to avenge her friends. Only the bars had kept her from a struggle to death.

That same innate impulse had resurfaced when she heard someone at the door. She was a hunted animal, eating on the run, clinging to the shadows, afraid to be seen, trusting no one, but she would fight for her life.

Was it just the adrenalin? Or was it something deeper and more ancient? A primal survival instinct. Long ago our ancestors came out of the jungle, Rosa thought. They brought their fears with them. They had seen ghosts in the dark primeval forests, heard the terrifying cries of animals who roamed the night. They created stories to describe their fears, stories which became myths and legends.

That ancient instinct is part of my heritage, she thought. She sniffed and was surprised how distinctly she could smell the sea. She could smell the aromas of food being prepared, the freshly oiled surface on the railings, the tinge of burning diesel fuel, the smoke that rose from the smokestack of the ship. Her hearing, too, was sharp, filtering sounds and identifying any that might pose a threat. From the deck below wafted the sounds of music.

"So, I am the hunter, and I am being hunted," she acknowledged to herself. "Just like some of the homies on the street. Now I know how it feels."

She finished her food and tossed the trash in a waste basket. Did I see the ChupaCabra in the cage because I wanted to see it? I believe it's there, and so it gathers power over me. If I allow it to control my life it can destroy me. That's what Uncle Billy told me: The evil is all around us and it's destroying so many. Like the drugs injected into the young. We need to fight back.

But now I need to hide, she thought, grabbing two more sandwiches and stuffing them into her jacket pocket. I need to hide until we reach L.A. She started down the outer walkway, searching for a safe place.

As she neared the center of the ship El Jefe emerged from a doorway and stood in front of her.

Rosa jumped with fright.

"Buenas tardes, Dr. Medina," he said. "I see you're out enjoying the night air."

Rosa froze. She looked down the deckway, but no help was in sight. El Jefe took a step forward.

"Yes, the night air can be very salubrious." He sneered. "Good for your health. But I hear we are approaching a storm. One has to be careful not to fall overboard when the storm rocks the ship."

He took another step forward, and Rosa inched back.

"You are not very talkative tonight," El Jefe continued. "I understand. You realize that you have mixed into business that is not yours. You are, perhaps, frightened. Well, I don't blame you. In fact, I warned you once about mixing in affairs that do not concern you. Now you must suffer the consequences."

Rosa turned to flee, but Detective Dill stepped out of the shadows. They had her trapped between them!

"There's no place to hide," Dill said, flashing a smile. "You see, we have been following you."

Both men advanced. Rosa glanced over the railing. Below her rolled the dark and silent sea, disturbed only by the slushing sound of the ship's wake. To jump into the water meant to drown.

"It's us or the ocean," Dill said. "You choose."

They closed in. Dill drew a pistol. Again she looked over the railing. If she gauged her jump correctly, she could land on top of one of the lifeboats that lined the deck below. If she missed she'd fall into the ocean.

Without hesitating she grabbed the rail and jumped. Her momentum sent her crashing on top of the canvas covering of a lifeboat, which broke her fall. Recovering from the rough landing, she jumped out of the boat onto the deck. She ran into the auditorium where the musical was just ending.

The finale included the entire cast of young women and men dressed in Uncle Sam outfits, ending the show with their rendition of "Yankee Doodle."

Rosa pushed her way through the crowd and worked her way toward the exit at the far end of the auditorium. The theater goers, mostly gray-haired retirees, had joined in raucously singing the last verse of the patriotic song. The auditorium reverberated with the music and loud chorus.

Rosa glanced back at the entrance. El Jefe stood outlined at the door, peering into the auditorium. She headed for the opposite exit, but Dill appeared there. There was no way out!

Rosa had surprised herself when she jumped over the railing to land on the lifeboat a deck below. Maybe her daily jogging and gym work had paid off. No, it was more than that. The instinct for survival had taken over and saved her. For the moment.

But now what?

The roaring crescendo of the song ended with streamers and confetti thrown at the audience by the players on stage. Strobe lights flashed across the audience as they sang the last bars of "Yankee Doodle." Red, white, and blue balloons and ribbons floated down from overhead.

The rousing song ended, the lights came on, and the MC took the microphone.

"Ladies and gentlemen, wasn't that a great show!"

The audience responded with enthusiastic cheering. Then the MC introduced, as a special treat, the captain of the ship. The captain rose to say a few words, thanking the actors and inviting everyone to a fabulous feast on the final night of their cruise.

The excited passengers clapped and hurried out of the auditorium, eager to get to the captain's party on the upper deck.

Rosa looked at the doors, which were still guarded. As the captain made his way by her, Rosa stepped alongside him and took his arm.

"Great show, wasn't it." She smiled.

The startled captain looked at her and frowned. "Yes, a great show. But I don't believe I've had the privilege, Ms.—"

"Rosa Medina," Rosa replied, as they walked out the door and past a very irritated Detective Dill.

CHAPTER TWENTY-EIGHT

"Rosa Medina," the captain repeated, glancing back at Dill. "You have a lot of spunk."

The captain, a heavy set man with a trim beard, smiled and bowed graciously at the passengers pressing around him and Rosa.

"And you have a monster loose on your ship," Rosa whispered.

"What kind of monster?"

"I think you know."

The captain paused, raised an eyebrow. "We should discuss this in my office," he said, clamping his hand over hers and turning her away from the crowd.

The group of elderly women anxiously waiting to escort him to the party pressed around them and blocked the way. They didn't like Rosa taking charge, and they would not be denied the captain's company.

"Captain! Captain!" a heavyset matron called, jostling forward. "You promised to join us."

"We won't go without you," another insisted, scowling at Rosa.

"Your fans call," Rosa said.

"You promised to sit at our table," the stout woman said as she took the captain's arm and tugged.

"Sorry I can't join you," Rosa whispered, firmly removing the captain's hand. She turned quickly and pushed her way through the crowd and down the stairs to the lower lobby. By the time Dill and El Jefe were able to follow she had disappeared.

Rosa knew she couldn't hide forever. Dill, Jefe, and Malorio were looking for her. The crowd attending the show had made it possible for her to escape, but after the party most would retire. She couldn't return to her room, and roaming around the ship she was sure to be spotted.

Time was running out.

So, thought Rosa, what do famous detectives do when all else fails? What would Lucha Corpi's woman investigator do? Or the hero of Manuel Ramos' murder mysteries set in Denver? Return to the scene of the crime, of course. Aboard ship the "scene of the crime" was the hold where the cargo of drugs were stored. And the beast.

Clinging to the shadows and using stairways reserved only for the ship's crew, Rosa made her way down into the bowels of the ship. She paused and sniffed the dank air of the cargo hold. Her skin tingled, warning caution. There it was again, a feeling from deep within, a survival instinct. The mild, often shy, professor of literature she had imagined herself to be had just jumped from one deck down onto a lifeboat and lived. She had the instinct to walk past Dill by taking the captain's hand. Now she had to ascertain the enemy's strategies before they found her.

What bravado! Even Nancy Drew wouldn't dare this. No, it wasn't foolhardiness. It went deeper than that. The skills that were surfacing had to do with staying alive. At every corner one of the dope smugglers might be waiting. Every resource she possessed had suddenly come alive. Faced with death, she vowed to live. She would reveal the murderers of her friends, and expose the cargo of despair they carried.

All she had to do was stay alive. Perhaps that's why she sniffed the air for signs of danger, cocked her ear to listen for the faintest footsteps.

Stealthily, she made her way in the cargo hold, weaving her way through the maze of crates that rose nearly to the roof of the large room. This was a labyrinth, and at every turn the Minotaur could be waiting. The Minotaur, the monster that was half man, half bull. For the ancient Greeks the monster lived in the labyrinth where heroes were tested. Today the monster lived in the maze of city streets, in the urban jungle. The streets were the labyrinth, the Minotaur was now the ChupaCabra!

Legends and myths tell us a great deal about our human nature, thought Rosa. Recently she had read a book suggesting that the ancient Mayas had a bat god, a god of death. He came to suffocate people, to draw the breath of life away. Was the ChupaCabra a god of death, like the bat god of the Mayas? Rosa made a mental note to do more research on the Mayan deity.

Suddenly she paused. Angry voices rang out ahead. Rosa approached cautiously.

Peering around the cartons of drugs she had explored earlier, she spied Dill and El Jefe arguing. A body lay on the floor.

"So where's Malo?" Dill asked.

"He's out there, looking for his monster," El Jefe replied.

"He's crazy! He can't control it. Look at what it did to Dago!"

Dago was the body on the floor. From where she stood Rosa could see the pool of blood.

"I'm crazy for trusting Malo," El Jefe said.

"Nobody can be trusted," Dill grunted.

"What are you saying? He set the beast loose to kill me? Is that it?" Jefe grabbed Dill by the collar.

"No, no! Relax. Malo will find his pet."

El Jefe pushed Dill aside. "I don't trust you hijos de la chingada!"

"Hey, you're overreacting. Relax—"

"I can't relax!" El Jefe shouted, wiping his sweating forehead. "Not with the ChupaCabra loose. Have you seen how it kills?"

"Hell no. I stayed clear," Dill replied.

"Malo keeps it in the cage, covered with a tarp. Nobody goes near it. You never sense the danger until it attacks."

"Are you saying we don't know what it looks like?"

"It stays in the dark. Maybe it can fly like a bat. When it strikes it fastens itself on the victim, like it did to Dago." He looked at the dead body.

"All I know is the damned thing stinks!" Dill cursed, glancing into the darkness of the hold.

"You smell it, then you have a few seconds before it eats your brains," Jefe said and took a pistol from his holster. "If I see it, I will kill it."

"Malo said bullets can't kill it."

"Bullshit! This will put a hole in it!"

"I don't think so. It's got to be something from the church, the natives at Lago Negro said. Maybe a stake in the form of a cross."

"You think the maldición is a vampire? Bullshit!"

"Suit yourself," Dill replied. "In the meantime what do we do with Dago?"

"Feed him to the sharks. Then we search for the girl."

"And toss her overboard," Dill said emphatically.

They put a tarp over the body, picked it up, and struggling with its weight they started toward the door. Rosa leaned back into the shadows, and as she did she pushed against a package which fell to the floor with a thud.

"What was that?" Dill asked, dropping the body.

"Maybe ChupaCabra," Jefe replied.

"Maybe it's the girl," Dill said. "Maybe we've found our little stowaway. You take that row."

They started toward the sound, pistols drawn. Rosa walked backward, not daring to breathe.

They came slowly down the two rows, blocking her exit and cornering her against the wall.

She glanced to both sides. There was no way out. She backed against the wall and waited. In the hold a gunshot wouldn't be heard. Then she and Dago's body would become shark meat.

Just as the two men were nearly upon her, Rosa felt the wall slide open. A hand clamped over her mouth, and someone pulled her into darkness.

CHAPTER TWENTY-NINE

"Shhhh," the man who held her whispered.

He had opened a secret door and pulled her into the engine room. He slid the door shut and waited.

Rosa held her breath. If the man was one of the conspirators she would be dead by now. The man held one hand over her mouth and a pistol in the other. Whoever it was had pulled her out of harm's way just in time.

The loud rumble of the motors suffocated most sounds. Still, she could hear Dill and El Jefe on the other side of the door.

"Nothing...our nerves."

"Damn! Let's get rid..."

The man held Rosa a few moments longer then slowly released his grip. "They're gone."

Rosa turned to face the man. He was elderly, with white hair and mustache, and he wore glasses.

"You saved my life," she whispered.

The man smiled.

Rosa looked closely. The man wasn't elderly. His grip was strong.

"Who are you?" Rosa asked, stepping back.

The man removed the thick glasses, pulled away the gray wig, then slowly peeled off the mustache.

In the dim light she could make out his face. "Bobby? Bobby Mejía?"

He smiled. "Who were you expecting, Eddie Olmos?"

"What the—"

"What the hell am I doing here? Chasing dope smugglers. And a bad cop."

"You know about the drugs?"

"Yes."

"And Detective Dill."

"We've known about him for some time. We knew the drugs were coming through a Mexican pipeline. But we didn't know how or where. Turns out our rotten cop paves the way for them. They truck the shipment right to a South Central warehouse. The same day, the drugs are out in the distribution system."

"How did you find out?"

"I followed you."

"Why?"

"You have something they want. Something so important it made Dill go after you."

"You believe he tried to run me over in Santa Fe?"

"Yes."

"Gracias," Rosa said, breathing a sigh of relief. She hadn't been imagining things.

"Have you figured out what they want?" Bobby asked.

Rosa told him about the photos José had taken, but she did not mention the photo of the beast.

"So that's the missing link!" Bobby exclaimed. "Are the photos good quality?"

"Yes. José had film for night photography. They're very clear. Both Malorio and Jefe are there."

"That will tie them to the drugs and José's death. José will be quite a hero."

"That's why I came after them," Rosa said. "I promised him."

"You kept your promise."

"Do you know about Malo?" she asked.

"Yes, Malo runs the whole show. From the poppy fields in Colombia to the marijuana plantations in Mexico, he controls a lot of territory. Now they're shipping in pseudoephedrine from Mexico and Asia. It's a multinational business making billions for the traffickers."

"And destroying lives," Rosa added. "Anyway, I have to thank you. If you hadn't been there—" She hated to think what Dill and El Jefe would have done to her.

"I've been watching them from here. It's a great observation post. So when I saw them coming for you, I did what comes naturally. Rescue the maiden."

So, even in difficult times the detective had a sense of humor. Rosa had to smile.

"This maiden thanks you. But what now? Are you the only police on board?"

"Yes. Dill doesn't know me, so I volunteered. I flew down on the same flight he was on. I followed him and saw them load the drugs on the ship, so here I am. They may know I'm on board, they just don't know what I look like. The disguise helped. I ran into one big problem: somebody stole my radio from my room. Now I need to get hold of a radio."

"You can't go to the captain. He's with them."

"Yeah, I know. They pay him off and smooth the way for the delivery."

"What do we do?"

"We hide till we dock in L.A. In the meantime, we try to find a radio."

"My cell phone!" Rosa exclaimed and dug it out of her pocket.

"We're out of range," Bobby replied, but he tried it anyway.

"No luck. Come on."

He led her through the entrails of the ship, the hissing of water pipes, the steady booming of the ship's propellers as they churned through the dark water.

They emerged through a door that led past the laundry area and up into the main deck.

"Why is it so dark?" Rosa asked.

Bobby paused. "The ship's lights are out."

The lobby was shrouded in darkness; so were the deckways. The ship was moving forward in the water, but it was a ghost ship. The electrical system was out.

Bobby opened the door to the upper deck foyer. A couple standing by the door jumped with fright.

"Oh, you scared the living daylights out of me!" a woman with a Texas drawl exclaimed.

"Sorry," Bobby apologized. "What happened?"

"Power outage," the man replied.

"And someone died," his wife added. "Stroke. Poor man."

"Where?" Bobby asked.

"Upstairs. It must have happened while we were at dinner. When the musicians went up they found him."

Bobby and Rosa hurried upstairs. They found passengers standing around the body.

"Who is it?"

"Anyone know him?"

"Nope."

"The doctor said he had a stroke..."

The small combo that was scheduled to play for the dance stood uneasily by their instruments, smoking cigarettes and looking toward the middle of the floor where the ship's doctor and his nurse had just covered the body. Two attendants stood by with flashlights in their hands.

"I'm going to have a look," Bobby said and pushed through the onlookers. "What happened?" he asked the doctor.

The doctor, startled by the question, answered. "Stroke victim. Nothing to worry about. Please stay back—"

"It may be my father," Bobby said. "He wasn't in his room. May I look?"

"No, it's not your father," the doctor said. "Please step back. We have to clear the area."

"I insist," Bobby demanded. "He's missing, and I just have to make sure."

Irritated, the doctor nodded at the nurse who pulled back the sheet and held a flashlight to the dead man's face. Bobby knelt. The vacant, terror-stricken eyes of El Jefe stared up at him.

"Not your father," the doctor said.

"No," Bobby replied. But it was not a stroke that killed El Jefe. His hair was clotted with blood.

"Thank you," Bobby said and returned to Rosa.

"El Jefe. Bled to death," he said and touched his head.

"ChupaCabra," Rosa whispered.

At that moment the voice of the captain came over the loudspeakers.

"Ladies and gentlemen. This is the captain speaking. As you know we are experiencing a slight problem with our electrical system. I want to assure you the ship is absolutely safe, and we are on our scheduled route to Los Angeles. The power outage affected only our lights. The motor and all the safety equipment is operating well. The outage does not compromise the safety of the vessel, but it may make it difficult for you to find your dance partners."

He chuckled and the passengers laughed uneasily.

"In order to give you more complete information," the captain continued, "we want you to report to your life stations. Each one of you is to report to the safety station you were assigned when we held the lifeboat drill. There you will be given flashlights and more specific instructions. Go slowly; there is no need to hurry. The stairs are dark and the elevators do not work. Please cooperate as we try to solve this problem."

People began to move toward their assigned stations.

"One more thing," the captain added. "There has been an unfortunate incident on the upper deck. I regret to inform you that a man has died of a stroke. This is not related to the light situation. I repeat, you are in no danger. Thank you for your cooperation."

Rosa looked at Bobby. Both knew the lights going out had something to do with the ChupaCabra. So did El Jefe's violent death.

CHAPTER THIRTY

osa and Bobby followed the passengers down the stairs.

"Why would they kill Jefe?" Rosa asked.

"Hard to say," Bobby replied. "Maybe they just want him out of the way. They're getting close to home, so one less partner means more money for the others. Happens in the drug world."

"Or the beast is loose, and nobody can control it."

Bobby nodded. "Yes. But with the photos you have, we'll be able to put this bunch away. You've done a lot of good, Rosa."

He squeezed her hand and looked at her with admiration.

"Thanks. I did it for my friends. But where do we go from here?"

"I need to get hold of a radio—"

He was interrupted by the doctor who had caught up with them. "Excuse me, may I have a word with you. I'm Dr. Vork, I have to talk to you." He spoke with a foreign accent.

Bobby glanced at Rosa.

"It's about the dead passenger," the doctor continued. "He didn't die of a stroke, did he?"

"No," Bobby replied.

"I examined him closely. There are puncture wounds on his skull. Most unusual. The wounds are not from a fall. You knew the man, did you not?"

"No," Bobby replied.

"But you inquired about him?"

"Let me level with you, doc," Bobby said. He showed him his badge, explained who he was, and gave enough details to draw the doctor into his confidence.

"Incredible," the doctor answered. "I find it hard to believe. What do you call this monster?"

"ChupaCabra," Rosa answered.

"I am afraid my Spanish is not good. What does it mean?"

Rosa explained. "It means goatsucker. This one doesn't kill goats, it sucks the life out of people."

"I can't believe such monsters exist. And drugs aboard ship—it is just too much! And you say the captain is implicated."

"Yes," Bobby replied. "Can we trust you?"

"But of course. I have only one concern, the well-being of the passengers and the crew. And I am certainly opposed to illegal drugs. In fact, I am shocked. And the captain...I am...astounded."

"Then help us," Bobby said. "The DEA and the Coast Guard are standing by, but I need a radio. Do you have access to one?"

"Yes. I have one in my office. I use it to confer with a hospital in Los Angeles when the need arises. Will it help?"

"Yes. I need to get the Coast Guard on board right away. We need a lot of help."

"I understand," the doctor replied. "Please follow me to my office."

Rosa and Bobby followed the doctor down a flight of stairs, then down a narrow hallway. The doctor's flashlight lit the way, probing the darkness like a stiff finger. As they entered the office, he pointed the beam toward a radio on the counter.

Bobby paused. "Pendejo," he muttered. He knew he had made a mistake.

149

"What?" the doctor asked.

"You knew I wasn't related to the dead man . . . "

"I only guessed," the doctor replied.

"You're with them," Bobby said, reaching for his pistol.

"Bobby!" Rosa cried, but too late. The door of the adjoining room burst open and a man with a gun appeared. He placed the muzzle of the pistol at the back of Bobby's head.

"Don't make any sudden moves, amigo," the man said, reaching for Bobby's pistol.

Rosa whirled to face Detective Dill.

"Dill!"

"Yours truly," Dill replied. "And you must be Mejía. Yeah, I recognize you now."

"Take them out!" the doctor interrupted. "Get rid of them. They know!"

"Relax, doc. I get rid of them in my own time."

"Should have known you'd buy the doc," Bobby said.

"In this business you have to pave a lot of paths," Dill said with a shrug. "Now sit. Tie them up, Doc." Rosa and Bobby sat, and the doctor taped their hands behind their backs.

Dill lit a cigarette. "So you teamed up with the girl. The famous professor who hunts the ChupaCabra. Lady, if you knew what that beast can do, you would have stayed clear."

"Leave her out of this," Bobby said. "Deal with me."

"Deal with you? Hey, I'm the one holding the gun."

"But he said the Coast Guard is waiting for the ship!" the doctor exclaimed.

"Bullshit," Dill replied. "Scare tactics." He turned to Bobby. "I know you've been following me for some time. Well, it doesn't matter now. In a few hours we dock. I collect and fly away. From L.A. harbor to LAX and Brazil in one easy day."

"You're a rotten cop!" Bobby challenged him.

Dill struck out, slapping him hard across the face. Blood spurted at Bobby's lip.

"He's also a coward!" Rosa exclaimed. She struggled to stand, but Dill pushed her back down.

"But I'm in charge! Say what you want."

"Why?" Bobby asked. "Why sell out and put all that poison in the streets?"

"Poison?" Dill said sarcastically. "It's not poison, detective, it's sugar. Sugar for the little monkeys who live in the street. They want the sugar, I supply it. You know, being a cop has no rewards. We work with the scum of the earth for little pay, then we get booted out and nobody gives a damn. Around us those that claim to be upholders of the law are getting rich. Why shouldn't I?"

"Only one reason," Rosa replied. "The money you make is blood money. It kills millions on the streets."

"Crack and meth suck the brains dry, is that it?" Dill replied. "I've heard all the excuses. I put twenty years in the force, so don't lecture me. They want the drugs, so I'm just doing them a favor by delivering. Right, Doc?"

The doctor smiled. "We do a big favor to society. Deliver drugs to the doorstep." Both laughed.

"So can the lectures!" Dill said and turned to the doctor. "I'm going for Malorio. Then these two go for a swim. In the meantime, keep an eye on them."

He took Bobby's pistol and the flashlight and went out.

"How many people aboard ship have you bribed?" Bobby asked.

"Enough to get the job done," the doctor replied.

"This isn't the only ship you use, is it?"

The doctor smiled. "This is big business. We bring in drugs, we bring in money to be laundered. Los Angeles is, how do you say, our capital." He laughed.

"But it can't last."

"Ah, you're wrong. As long as there is hunger for drugs we make money. We are not afraid of the police. For a while our competitors were the crazy kids who learned to make meth in their bathtubs at home. But the feds made methamphetamine illegal, then they shut down ephedrine. We learned to supply pseudo. We ship pseudoephedrine in from Asia. Tons of it. But we also supply high-quality heroin. There will always be a market, and people willing to be bought, as you say. We had information from inside the police department that you were after us. So we simply maneuver around the opposition. Like a chess game."

"Why get rid of Jefe?"

The doctor shrugged. "It was an accident."

Rosa sniffed the air. It was suddenly there, the faint sulfur smell that came with the ChupaCabra. She stiffened then glanced at Bobby. He, too, had smelled the odor.

There followed a scratch at the door. The doctor looked at the door. "That you Dill?" he called. "Malorio?"

A louder thump followed. The doctor went to the door. "Frank? Malo?"

There was no answer, only a louder thump.

The doctor opened the door slowly, peered into the dark hallway then stepped out. He disappeared suddenly, uttering a gut-wrenching cry.

The door swung shut. Outside Bobby and Rosa heard a second scream, then silence. They looked at each other. The ChupaCabra had struck.

The scratching at the doorknob resumed. The ChupaCabra was loose. The traffickers had used it to kill El Jefe, and now it had killed the doctor.

They were next.

CHAPTER THIRTY-ONE

The door rattled again.

"There's a knife in my pocket!" Rosa cried.

Both stood and Bobby reached for her pocket. "Can't get to it," he replied. He meant not in time. Whatever was at the door had super-human strength. It had pulled the doctor out of the room and was now ready to break down the door.

Another loud rattle shook the door, followed by a loud eerie grunt. The monster had them cornered.

"The fire extinguisher!" Rosa said, nodding at the extinguisher at the foot of the doctor's desk.

"Right!" Bobby replied. Would the sodium bicarbonate turn back the beast? It was all they had.

He crouched and picked up the extinguisher. "Pull the pin!"

Rosa reached for the pin and pulled it. She screamed as the door suddenly flew open and two eyes blazed in the dark. The huge shadow of the ChupaCabra stood outlined at the door.

"Aim the nozzle!" Bobby shouted.

Rosa aimed the nozzle at the dark shape.

Struggling to hold the extinguisher with his hands tied, Bobby pressed the lever and a huge cloud of whooshing foam shot out. A terrifying scream filled the room as the spray hit the beast's eyes. Crying in pain, it retreated.

They heard it slouching down the hallway, and waited with bated breath. They peered into the dark. It was gone.

Rosa whispered, "Thank God."

Bobby dropped the extinguisher. "You can say that again."

"Its eyes," she whispered. "All I could see were the eyes of fire...."

"There's a pair of scissors on the desk," Bobby said and fumbled about until he reached them. Slowly and meticulously he cut at Rosa's tape. When he was done she freed him. "You okay?" he asked, placing his hands on her shoulders.

"Yes. Sorry about the scream."

"Hey, you thought of the extinguisher. That saved us." He paused. "They want you out of the way."

Rosa nodded. "I think the ChupaCabra has me on its hit list."

"I'm sorry I doubted you. Working the streets makes me a realist. But I've never seen anything like that."

Just then the ship groaned and lurched forward, and Bobby reached out to keep her from falling.

"What was that?"

"The ship hit something," Bobby said. "Come on!"

He grabbed her hand and they rushed out the door, past the doctor's body, and down the dark hallway. They climbed the stairs to the main deck. The passengers, who had huddled for hours at their safety stations, had rushed to the railings.

"What happened?" Bobby asked the first man they encountered.

"Somebody said we hit a whale," the man replied. "And so near port. I don't get it."

He pointed. In the distance they could see the lights of Los Angeles and its sister communities spread against the vague

served within the hour. I hope you enjoy this last breakfast with us. In the meantime, enjoy the whales."

"About time they got the electricity back," a woman scoffed as she stomped away. "I need my coffee."

"You're always complaining," her husband said, following her.

Rosa turned to Bobby. "Maybe the whales are here for another reason."

"What?"

"They sense what's on board the ship."

He nodded. He was a realist, but he had just faced a danger he had never faced before. On the streets of L.A. he could handle any situation, but the beast with the burning eyes that had just attacked them was something out of a bad fantasy. But fantasy had not killed the doctor. The beast had. It was real.

"We have to stop the drugs...We have to find Malorio," Rosa said.

"They're armed, I'm not," he reminded her. "Besides, in a couple of hours we dock. DEA and federal marshals will be waiting."

"What if they have an escape route?" she asked.

Before he could answer someone shouted "Look!"

The whales rose in unison, breaking the surface of the water, then diving they disappeared, leaving in their wake a deep silence. The sea grew calm, a silver slate, an element of mystery that was life itself.

In all this beauty lives the ChupaCabra, Rosa thought. It's still out there.

CHAPTER THIRTY-TWO

"Can Malorio control ChupaCabra?" Bobby asked.

"Maybe he never did," Rosa replied. "ChupaCabra is bigger than any one man. ChupaCabra attacks the vulnerable. But why kill Jefe and the doctor?"

"Drug dealers turn against each other," Bobby replied. "Whoever controls the ChupaCabra owns the drug shipment. That means money and power. They kill whoever gets in the way."

"And the electrical outage?"

"Seems like Dill would want the ship to enter port quietly. A normal cruise. Now they have a problem on their hands. Or maybe it's part of their plan."

"What do you mean?"

He pointed toward the lifeboats. Two men were removing the canvas coverings from a lifeboat.

"They transfer the drugs to the lifeboats. Customs checks the cruise ships and find nothing. In the smaller boats they can transport the drugs into private docks anywhere along the coast. Stay and watch what they load. I'm going back to use the doctor's radio."

Rosa nodded, called "be careful," and watched him disappear into the milling crowd. The scene with the whales had been a temporary respite. Now an anxious feeling spread through the crowd of passengers. Crew members were stopped and asked what was going on, but they knew nothing.

"Stay by the boats."

"Keep your life jackets on."

"This drill is part of the program before we dock."

"The captain will make an announcement any time now."

The responses from the crew didn't satisfy the passengers. Those who had been on prior cruises realized something wasn't right. Anxiety grew as the ship seemed to drift.

Rosa waited as long as she could. Something told her Bobby was in trouble. Maybe he had run into the captain and was a prisoner. Or he would retrieve his pistol and in order to keep her out of harm's way he would go after Dill alone. She had to get to the cargo hold.

She crossed the lobby and found the stairs that led below. She stole along in darkness until she entered the hold. Cautiously, she made her way through the maze of stacked crates.

She stopped when she recognized Dill's voice.

"Damn you, Malo! If it wasn't for your monster we wouldn't be in this mess!"

"Damn yourself, gringo!" Malorio countered. "It was your idea to get rid of Jefe."

"Your beast's gone wild. Now the doc's dead!"

Malorio laughed. "That leaves more money for us. Don't worry, my pet is in the cage."

Rosa crept as close as she dared. Inching along the rows of crates she backed into a space between two containers. From here she could observe the two.

"I don't like it!" Dill exploded. "We're this close to unloading the shipment and your ape is killing people!"

"Ape?" Malo laughed. "You think the ChupaCabra is an ape? Estás pendejo!"

"I'm not a fool!" Dill retorted. "I know exactly what I'm doing. I sacrificed a lot for this shipment, and I'm not giving it up!"

"Pinche, buey," Malorio replied. "I know what I'm doing. Today, ChupaCabra strikes L.A. Plenty of cocaina for los ricos! Crystals for the homeboys!"

His laughter echoed through the maze of containers. Rosa could tell both men were high on something. But she was so intent on listening that she didn't notice the acrid smell that touched her nostrils until it was too late. A claw-like hand reached out and gripped her shoulder, digging deep into the flesh.

Rosa cried in pain and turned to look into the horrifying face of ChupaCabra. She had backed up against the cage that held the beast.

"Did you hear that!" Dill shouted, instantly reaching for his pistol.

Malorio nodded. "La muchacha!"

He too drew a pistol, and both men stumbled down the row of crates toward Rosa. Behind her the ChupaCabra raised a high-pitched, murderous scream. It had drawn blood; now its need was to kill.

Rosa cringed. The men who wanted her dead loomed in front of her. Behind her rose the murderous shape of the ChupaCabra.

"There!" Dill pointed.

"The curse of el ChupaCabra destroys everyone in its path!" Malorio called. "You cannot escape!"

For a split second Rosa couldn't move. The end was coming and it seemed to be happening in slow motion. The pistols pointed at her would fire at any moment; behind her the claws of the ChupaCabra reached out through the bars of the cage.

Then her survival instinct took over. She turned, pulled the latch, and flung the door open. She jumped aside as the beast went flying out, straight at Dill and Malorio. They cried out and fired wildly as ChupaCabra descended on them.

A terrified Rosa looked on as the beast tore into the two men. Almost as soon as the attack began, it was over. Their screams stopped as the two men went down in a pool of blood.

Those who lived by the curse of the ChupaCabra had died under its influence. The attack had been so sudden and vicious that they had no defense against the beast. But their stray bullets had done damage, puncturing the oil containers along the wall. Suddenly a ball of flame exploded.

Looming over the dead bodies, the ChupaCabra rose to its full height. It turned to face Rosa. Outlined against the roaring fire, it was the image of an evil force bent on destroying the world.

"Virgen María!" Rosa cried and reached for Father Larry's knife. She pushed the blade open and held the knife out the way a priest might hold a cross to exorcise the devil. She was ready to die fighting.

The ChupaCabra hesitated. Its blood-curdling cry echoed in the burning room, but it didn't attack. The young woman held a power the beast could not defeat. With a final scream it turned and disappeared into the black smoke.

Rosa stood transfixed. She could hear her heart pumping; her knees felt weak. She realized she had beaten the curse of the ChupaCabra. It could not harm her, and in the future she would let everyone know there was a way to defeat the curse.

The real threat was the fire. As it spread, it heated up other containers of oil, which exploded and added to the raging inferno. The only way out of the hold was through the secret door Bobby had used before. She found the door and pushed, but it wouldn't open. No matter how hard she heaved, the door remained sealed. Behind her a new explosion rocked the hold, and the intense smoke choked her.

Gathering the last of her strength she pushed one more time and the door slid open. She fell through the threshold into Bobby's arms.

"Bobby! Thank God!"

He pulled her to the side, raised his pistol, and peered into the burning room.

"They're all dead!" Rosa shouted.

Bobby held Rosa around the waist and helped her out of the engine area and up a staircase to the lower deck. When they came upon a fire alarm, he broke the glass and pulled the handle. Instantly the alarm went off, echoing down the corridor.

By the time they reached the main deck, pandemonium had broken out. Passengers were heading for the lifeboats. Already black smoke was rising into the sky.

The first officer's voice boomed above the fire alarm siren.

"Ladies and gentlemen, we believe we have a fire on board. We are checking the situation. Don't panic. The alarm may be a false. We are taking the precaution of getting you aboard the lifeboats. Please go to your assigned boat area. Please follow your drill captain."

"They believe we have a fire?" a man in front of Rosa cried. "What do they call that?"

He pointed at the column of smoke billowing into the morning sky.

"Fire!" another man shouted, and the passengers rushed toward the lifeboats. Crew members did their best to control the crowd.

Rosa and Bobby donned the life vests a crew member tossed their way and waited in line to board. The first officer continued giving instructions over the loudspeaker, explaining that things were under control.

"Ladies and gentlemen, the Coast Guard has been alerted. It's on its way. Please continue boarding the lifeboats in an orderly manner. The fire is restricted to the hold. Our fire team has it under control. We have plenty of time to evacuate the ship."

The first lifeboat hit the water with a splash, amid shouts and screams. By the time Rosa and Bobby's boat was launched, the column of black smoke was shooting into the sky. The first tongues of flame licked through the smokestack. The fire had not been contained.

Coast Guard ships, sirens blasting, plowed toward the ship. A couple of Navy helicopters buzzed overhead. Other ships in the area had turned to assist. Even in the confusion, everyone had made it safely off the ship.

The lifeboats turned in the direction of the Los Angeles port, leaving behind them a burning ship. Rosa sat huddled in Bobby's arms. She felt safe with him. The thought of not being able to escape the burning room made her shiver.

"That's twice you came to my rescue. I owe you."

"No, we owe you Rosa. You led us to the drugs. Now they're going into the ocean. I think I'll recommend you for a medal."

Rosa smiled and turned to look at the burning ship. What of the ChupaCabra? Would the beast go down with the ship, or would it find a way to slouch once again toward the barrios of the people? One multi-million-dollar drug shipment would go to the depths of the sea, but tomorrow those who profited from destroying minds would be planning a new shipment.

How could those hooked on drugs find a way to beat the vicious craving that destroyed body and soul? Perhaps the answer lay partly in the teachings of the ancestors. The elders taught that when neighbors lived in harmony with each other, everyone prospered. But different forces rose to destroy the harmony of communities. Mind-destroying drugs were just one of those terrible forces in the world.

There is a path to follow, Rosa thought. But she didn't want to travel alone. She looked at Bobby.

"When this is over I want to visit Uncle Billy and Indio. Visit my family in Santa Fe. Would you like to go with me?"

"I've never been to New Mexico," Bobby replied. Then after a pause he added, "But I have a feeling I'm going to learn a lot about you and your part of the country."

Rosa smiled and leaned into his embrace.

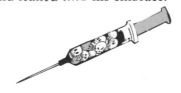

CHAPTER THIRTY-THREE

Rosa sat in the small barrio theater enjoying the last scene of the play. The actors were doing a great job, and Eddie's directing was superb.

"Aren't they fabulous?" she whispered to Bobby.

"You bet." He squeezed her hand and looked at the bandage on Rosa's shoulder. "Hurt?"

"No," she replied. "It's healing. Tomorrow I can remove the bandage."

The doctor had told her the scratch would heal and leave a scar. A reminder of her struggle against the curse of the ChupaCabra.

"You're quite a woman," he said.

"Gracias. You're quite a man."

"I would say we fit."

Rosa nodded. "Yes, we fit."

Like two actors on the stage of life they had shared an adventure, and thus found each other. So different, and yet so alike. But that's the way it was, Rosa had discovered. Every single moment changed your life, revealing truths you could never imagine. Yes, she and Bobby were like actors on a stage moving back and forth toward an evolving destiny.

Community theater at its finest, thought Rosa. There's a lot of talent in the barrio, and it could blossom if only the resources were available. The unleashing of all that positive energy could counteract the cancer of illegal drugs.

The barrios of L.A., she had learned from living in California, represented islands of possibility. Caught between the world of Anglo America and the Latino world of the south, the barrios were a new frontier. That border could become a new world community where north and south met; or it could disintegrate into a zone of fear if Latinos were used as scapegoats. The barrios from California to Texas represented a new potential. The border could be bridged, or it could become a wall of separation. Hope lay in people's willingness to live as neighbors. Brave new worlds could evolve where the cultures of the world met. Have we outgrown words like *love* and *harmony*? thought Rosa. What of understanding, sharing, learning?

Latin Americans seeking a better life in el norte were no different from the American pioneers who had ventured west in the nineteenth century. All were trespassers on original Native American soil. Migrations were as old as the history of humans on earth. Immigrants sought a place to work, build homes, and provide for families. All came with a dream. Often old prejudices stood in the way, and those in power held control over the lives of the oppressed.

Now she knew from firsthand experience much of the drug problem revolved around power. Those in power needed to keep an oppressed underclass. And education was a way out of that oppression.

She glanced at Cristina, who smiled and gave her an old barrio sign. Rosa smiled. Next to her sat Leo and Mousey. They were enjoying the play. Months ago they wouldn't have thought of attending a play, and here they sat, awed by the power of the story and the actors, hanging on every word of the drama. Yes, it was possible.

A few rows down Eddie sat with Tony García and Cici Aragón, special guests. Playwrights and actors spreading a message of hope in the Latino barrios. Eddie glanced at Rosa and winked. They had met in the lobby before the performance, and Eddie had invited Rosa and her friends to the cast party after the play. He wanted to hear about the cruise ship. The L.A. and national media had publicized the event, and Rosa was sought after for a story. But she had kept to herself.

Eddie wanted to turn her story into a play about ChupaCabra.

"Better than Frankenstein or the werewolf," he had announced dramatically. "This is a real Latino monster!"

Rosa had smiled. Yes, Latinos had their heroes in books and movies, heroes who battled the monsters in the folktales of the people. But la Llorona and the Cucúi were getting old. What was needed to reflect the fears and concerns of the people was a new blood-thirsty beast. ChupaCabra.

Rosa smiled with satisfaction and held Bobby's hand. She felt comfortable with him. He had asked her to meet his parents. Everything was clicking in the right places. Was she falling in love?

The image of the burning cruise ship crossed Rosa's thoughts. All of the passengers had reached shore safely, but the captain was not accounted for. Had he gone down with the ship? Had his greed driven him into the fire to try to save the drugs? Or had he met ChupaCabra? No one would ever know.

Rosa couldn't stop wondering why the ChupaCabra had turned away from her. Was it the cross on the knife that saved her? Or was being willing to fight the beast enough to overcome its threat? She had taught her students that they could all become warriors as they found their own identities and potential. They could all become warriors in a social struggle. Drugs would only keep them from their true path. Had she become a warrior woman? Was her spirit strong enough to continue to fight the ChupaCabra? Other Latinas would help: Cristina, Leo, mothers from the barrios, poets, writers, educators. Whoever said *Si se puede!* was right. It could be done!

And it helped to have a partner for the road ahead. Bobby had insisted they attend the play. He had taken her, Leo, and Mousey to dinner.

"You need to take your mind off what happened," he said. He was a great dinner companion, humorous, with a hundred stories to tell. The kids loved him.

"I didn't know cops could be funny," Leo said later as they freshened up in the bathroom. "And he's cute. He likes you, profe."

Rosa laughed. Yes, she admitted to herself, I like him too.

Now she had to think of the future. Spring break had come and gone, and tomorrow she would meet her classes. A bit unprepared, to be sure, but she was eager to get back in the swing of things. Could she tell her students about how she spent her spring break? Perhaps the study of literature would pale in comparison. How could she lecture on folklore, mythology, and feminism when her mind was still on the recent events? She would be thinking of José, Herminio, and Chuco for a long time.

The cruise ship had gone to the bottom of the sea, so the streets of the city would never see the drugs that were destroyed. But Rosa was realistic enough to know that a new ship was even now cruising toward L.A. Those who made money from selling illegal drugs would figure out a way to get the brain-sucking drugs into the country.

She had helped stop one shipment, but chasing drug dealers wasn't her real calling. She had to follow her destiny, her fate. She was a teacher. She knew she was good at bringing her love of literature to her students. Yes, she could do that. Inspire them.

People everywhere continued to invent new stories. The witches and monsters of prior ages still lived in the stories of her community. She would tell her students stories about la Llorona and the Cucúi. Then she would tell them stories of the ChupaCabra and how it prowled the streets of the urban jungle. These stories were not composed by academics, they were told by the people.

Over a backyard fence a man would tell his neighbor: "Sabes que? My compadre found two of his chickens dead in his back yard. No, not by dogs. Their blood was sucked out. Sí, like a vampire. Know what I think? ChupaCabra is in our neighborhood."

And so a story would evolve and spread. That's the way it had always been. Rosa smiled. She had faith in the people. But suddenly she felt uneasy. The wound on her shoulder itched.

She looked out the side door that had been left open for fresh air. A breeze rippled through the trees and bushes outside. Rosa peered into the darkness. She felt a tingle along her spine. The beast was moving through the streets of the city. It was out there, somewhere. Where would it strike next?